Praise for

POWDER MONKEY

Adventures of a Young Sailor

A NCSS-CBC Notable Social Studies Trade Book for Young People

"Readers will be absorbed in the day-to-day life of young Sam, and his vivid tale will keep them on edge as he tries to escape his commission. . . . Not for the faint of heart, this novel is a brilliant introduction to the likes of C. S. Forester's classic 'Horatio Hornblower' saga."
—*SLJ*

"Readers who prefer their wooden decks awash in blood 'and worse' will not be disappointed. . . . Voracious fans of the nautical genre will happily sign on."
—*Kirkus Reviews*

"Fans of the *Master and Commander* series or movie will enjoy this seafaring adventure. Sam is an engaging narrator who includes tremendous detail about daily life aboard ships."
—*VOYA*

"Sam leads an exciting and dangerous life as a powder monkey. . . . A gripping adventure story on the high seas."
—Travelforkids.com

Adventures of a Young Sailor

POWDER MONKEY

Paul Dowswell

BLOOMSBURY

Published by Bloomsbury Publishing, New York, London, and Berlin
Distributed to the trade by Holtzbrinck Publishers

The Library of Congress has cataloged the hardcover edition as follows:
Dowswell, Paul.
Powder monkey : [adventures of a young sailor] / by Paul Dowswell. — 1st U.S. ed.
p. cm.
Summary: Thirteen-year-old Sam endures harsh conditions, battles, and a shipwreck after being
pressed into service aboard the HMS *Miranda* during the Napoleonic Wars.
ISBN-10: 1-58234-675-5 • ISBN-13: 978-1-58234-675-5 (hardcover)
1. Great Britain—History, Naval—19th century—Juvenile fiction. [1. Great Britain—History,
Naval—19th century—Fiction. 2. Napoleonic Wars, 1800-1815—Fiction. 3. Sea stories.] I. Title.
PZ7.D7598Po 2005   [Fic]—dc22   2005013049

ISBN-10: 1-58234-748-4 • ISBN-13: 978-1-58234-748-6 (paperback)

Typeset by Dorchester Typesetting Group Ltd.
Printed in the U.S.A. by Quebecor World Fairfield
1 3 5 7 9 10 8 6 4 2

Bloomsbury Publishing, Children's Books, U.S.A.
175 Fifth Avenue, New York, NY 10010

All papers used by Bloomsbury Publishing are natural, recyclable products made from wood grown
in well-managed forests. The manufacturing processes conform to the environmental regulations of
the country of origin.

To
J & J
D & B
and
CV

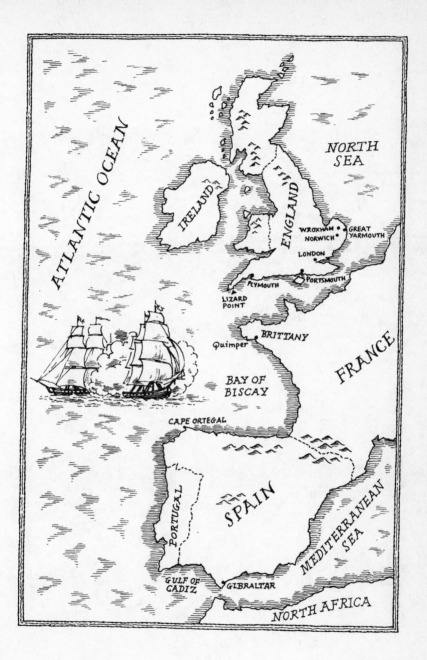

Contents

Contents

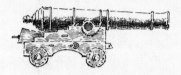

I have watched great men-o'-war raked and blazing, their crews scurrying like ants before the white-hot beam of a child's sun glass. I have seen boys and men right beside me, torn in two halves by chain shot, bloodied torsos twitching in death spasm, faces all around staring in wide-eyed horror. I have looked on broken ships swallowed by the sea, silhouetted in the dusk of a pale pink sky. I have known the bile-sour taste of fear, and I have cried with such relief I felt faint with joy. And all these things I knew before I turned fourteen.

Samuel Witchall is my name. I was born in 1787, in the village of Wroxham, in Norfolk. Stay with me, and I will tell you a story you will never forget . . .

CHAPTER 1

Drawn to the Sea

One night at supper I told my father I wanted to become a sailor. He laughed at first, not taking me seriously. But when I insisted, his face grew darker.

'The Navy's a brutal calling, Sam, only suitable for brutal men. You're a thinker, you're a sensitive boy, and you're still young, for heaven's sake. I'll not have you waste your talents with the thugs and sweepings of our gaols that fill the Navy ships.' Then his voice softened. 'Besides – I want to see you grow up and marry. I want you to look after your mother and me in our old age! We don't want you getting yourself killed hundreds of miles away from home.'

My mother stayed silent, but her eyes filled with tears. There had been four of us boys once, rather than two. Smallpox carried off my two younger brothers when I was six. Now there was just my older brother Thomas and me. He was more of a timid soul and not so interested in the world. It was Tom who would inherit my father's shop. My father had in mind that I would teach at the village school and help my uncle run his shop. A life selling groceries would suit Tom fine. But not me. I always wanted to escape from the vast, flat horizon of Norfolk, with only the flapping sails of a few creaking windmills to break the silence. Grey and grim it is for two-thirds of the year, with a biting wind coming straight off the North Sea. Reverend Chatham, our village parson, says there are barely three hundred people in the parish. Imagine just seeing those same few faces for the rest of your life?

My older cousin John had sailed a merchantman from London to Madagascar, then through the Indian Ocean. He came back berry-brown, cock o' the walk. What tattoos he had – beautiful curling designs up his right arm, that the natives had done when the ship stopped in Sumatra. I wanted to see the things he'd seen.

Recently my father and I had visited relatives close by Lowestoft. I wandered down to the beach with my cousin Joe and stared out to sea. The waves were high and crashed noisily on to the beach, and I was filled with excitement. Then, as we stood there, running up and down in the sand every so often to keep warm, a flotilla of British warships sailed by in the middle distance. I asked to borrow Joe's 'bring 'em near', what he called his telescope. These ships looked magnificent – great, bruising war machines, bristling with gun ports, and with masts that reached impossibly high. Peering through the eyepiece I could see the officers in their blue coats, and men and boys scurrying up the rigging with great speed and daring.

My father and I argued for weeks about what I should do. Eventually my parents agreed to help – but only on the condition that I joined a merchant ship, rather than the Royal Navy. I didn't mind. Although the fighting ships I had seen fired my imagination, I knew enough to believe life aboard them was quite as barbaric as my father had said.

'We've discussed the matter with Reverend Chatham,' said my father. 'He knows a merchant captain called Thomas Rushford in Great Yarmouth. He'll see if Rushford will have you as a ship's boy.'

A week after my thirteenth birthday Rushford agreed to take me at once into his ship the *Lady Franklyn*, which sailed the coastal routes of England and Wales. Sometimes, I was told, the *Franklyn* ventured further afield – north to the colder waters of Scotland, or far south into the Mediterranean. Once or twice, she had even braved the North Atlantic, with goods for Boston and New York. This sounded exactly like the ship for me.

My father took me to the *Franklyn* one late spring morning in 1800. She was a sturdy brig with two masts, and a black hull topped with a band of golden yellow around the gunnels. The crew numbered rarely more than fifteen or sixteen men. I was taken under the wing of the Captain's apprentice – a wiry boy a year or so older than me, with a handsome face and a shock of dark hair. He was called George Mansell. His father was a merchant who wanted one of his sons to become a sea captain.

We took slate from Wales to Bristol, to make the roofs of new houses in that ever-growing city, and ferried timber from Dorset to Whitby. I learned my trade quickly, which pleased Captain Rushford, and could soon tie knots and work ropes with the confidence of a born sailor. With a daily round of washing dishes and scrubbing the deck, my hands became as tough as leather, which made scurrying up the rigging easier. Cleaning clothes took place once a week, if that. It took me a full month to stop retching whenever I had to clean the clothes in the bucket of urine provided for that purpose, but, as the Captain occasionally reminded me, it got the dirt out like nothing else known to man.

Despite the chilly fogs and occasional rough seas, I took to life on ship with a pleasure I had never known before. When work was slack, and the sun shone brightly, I would climb to the top of the foremast, and, with my face full on to the wind, could make-believe I was flying over the sea like a great white gull. I loved the dawn and dusk best. On early-morning watches the sun would come up to burn away the mist over the cliffs, leaving a pure, clear light that would only grow hazy as the day grew hotter. Sunsets were extraordinary – especially when we were away from the coast, and there was nothing on either side of the ship save the flat canvas of the sea. Night would come in from the east like a vast dark blanket, and stray clouds would turn from light pinks to fiery reds against a milky-blue sky. Then I would go to my straw mattress – 'donkey's breakfast', the crew called them – in the forecastle, and sleep the sleep of the just. But this life I had chosen was about to be taken away from me.

The dawn of 27th August brought an unwelcome sight. As we sailed along the Dorset coast, a man high in the rigging spotted a French privateer closing in two miles to our stern. As he called down his voice betrayed his anxiety, and his fear lodged in my bones.

I was standing on the forecastle next to George

Mansell and gave him a puzzled look.

'Privateers,' he said. 'They're almost as bad as pirates.'

I must have still looked baffled, because his voice took on a slight impatience.

'They're armed ships given permission by their government to capture enemy vessels. She's going to try to seize us and take us back to France. We have privateers too, I'm afraid to say.'

Captain Rushford was roused from his cabin, and arrived on deck looking grim and determined. He studied the approaching ship for a couple of minutes, then gathered us together – all fifteen of us in varying shapes and sizes – and made a short speech.

'We must with all haste empty our hold to try to gain speed. The wind is fair, and we may yet outrun our pursuer. The ship's gun must remain on board, however, as I fear we will have to fight. With this in mind, when you have emptied the hold, you may be called to my cabin to be issued with cutlass, musket and pistol. I don't have to remind you of the fate of British merchantmen recently held prisoner in Quimper. Now carry on.'

George and I were confused by this last reference. One of the old salts filled us in. 'Couple o' thousand men died. They just let them waste away ... wicked business, it were.'

All available men went at once to the hold. While some of us set about draining the water barrels into the step of the main mast and pumping this overboard, others began to haul our cargo – sacks of cattle feed – over the side of the ship. It was hard, exhausting work, and as I tired I began to fret about the coming attack.

'Don't worry, laddie,' said Langan McKenzie, new to the ship and intending to work his way back in stages to Aberdeen, 'we'll speed up once this lot is gone.' But I suspected the Frenchman was light too, and her crew were obviously prepared for a fight.

As the hold emptied I did sense the *Franklyn* picking up speed. By midday I began to hope that we would outrun our pursuer. But by the mid-afternoon we could clearly see the ship was gaining on us. I began to realise we were not going to get away. Shortly before four o'clock Captain Rushford gathered us together and issued orders in an impressively workman-like manner.

'We must prepare for the worst, although we may yet outrun our enemy.' Then he spoke directly to his second-in-command – the ship's master Jeremiah Clay. 'Mr Clay, move the gun to the stern and man it with two men of your own choosing. The rest of you will arm yourselves and prepare to repel boarders.' He looked at George and me. 'Mansell and Witchall, you will remain below deck, and assist any injured man who may come for your help.'

I was greatly relieved that I was not expected to fight, but tried not to appear too pleased about it. I could see many of the crew looked quite sick with fear. Most of them were not trained fighters and obviously had no stomach for battle.

So George and I went below and waited. Neither said a word to the other, for we could scarcely believe what was happening. We had hoped to escape without a fight. Then, there was a loud bang off the starboard side of the ship, and an instant later the cabin wall in front of us disappeared in an explosion of splinters . . .

We were both blown off our feet by the force of the blast. When I recovered my senses I realised I was uninjured. The cannonball that had burst through the forecastle and then out the other side of the ship missed me by inches. George had not been so lucky. A jagged splinter of wood, the length and width of a man's hand, had embedded itself in his left arm. He immediately began to make a fearful wailing noise, yelping in agony, and went white with fear. His eyes, too, filled with tears. I had seen accidents with farm implements out in the fields around our village, so I knew a little of what to do. We were close to my bunk, and I ran to fetch a scarf of mine to tie tightly above the wound.

'Keep your injured arm held high above your head,' I told George, 'and come and sit down in this corner.' I was pleased to see that he was hardly bleeding. Then I ran to look for Captain Rushford, to ask for the key to the cupboard which held the ship's medicine chest. Out on deck I could see the privateer was almost upon us.

I found Rushford easily enough, and hurried up to the starboard side of the quarterdeck where he was standing. As I approached I realised he was straining to hear something being shouted over to us with a loud hailer from the privateer. I knew no French, so I could not understand what was being said. Then Rushford turned to speak to Jeremiah Clay and the *Franklyn*'s bosun, a Swede by the name of Filip Anders.

'He says, "Heave to, and let us board you. Surrender now and I promise you will be properly looked after."'

Anders and Clay were clearly not impressed by this information. All three of them began to argue heatedly. I began to feel very afraid and edged nearer to overhear. Rushford was speaking with commanding determination.

'We must surrender. There's no sense in sacrificing the lives of the crew in a battle we have no chance of winning. We're outnumbered and outgunned, and the Frenchman is faster than us.'

But Clay and Anders stood together, determined to fight. Pointing insolently at the Captain's chest Clay shouted, 'We can still have them if we put some guts into it. I'll be damned if I'm going to rot in some French prison for the next six years. I'd rather die now and be done with it.'

The conversation continued for a few moments, but

the wind snatched away the words. Mr Clay was known to the crew as a man of determined action and a regrettably short fuse. I had always tried to keep out of his way, as he showed little patience with novice sailors.

Now I watched in some trepidation as he returned to the gun which had been set up ready in the stern. By the way he walked I wondered if he had been drinking. Clay nodded to the seamen he had chosen to man the gun, and without a word they levered it round a few degrees with a handspike and then fired it.

The effect on the privateer – which we were now near enough to see was called the *Isabelle* – was spectacular. Our gun was loaded with chain shot – two heavy metal weights linked by a chain – which tumbled over almost too fast for the eye to see, breaking the mainsail yardarm from the foremast and tearing the canvas with an almighty rip.

I turned at once to Captain Rushford. He looked stunned. It had all happened in an instant, and now it was too late to do anything about it. The expression on his face quickly changed from surprise to open fury.

'Enjoy your triumph, Mr Clay,' he said. 'Now I doubt any of us shall live to see the evening.'

Yet when I turned my gaze to the *Isabelle* I could see Clay's shot had caused mayhem. The rigging around the foremast was torn and tangled, and men on deck were running around hastily trying to correct the sails. Clay and his crew were working feverishly at their gun, reloading it with another chain shot as quickly as they could.

Clay glanced over to the Captain with a look of impertinent glee. Rushford, his brow creased, his mouth open in disbelief, was now torn in his reactions. Perhaps Clay had been right to fire after all?

Almost at once the *Isabelle* began to veer away and drop behind. At this moment I allowed myself to believe that perhaps the *Franklyn* would escape after all. All hands waited for the privateer's response, expecting at least another cannonball to smash into our sides. But instead, the French ship raised a large red flag. A seaman next to me on the deck had an expression of sheer horror on his face. I asked what it meant.

'No quarter,' he said in disbelief. 'They're going to fight us to the death.'

Captain Rushford was standing alone, staring dumb-founded over the quarterdeck. I took my chance and went over to ask him for the key to the medicine chest.

'Yes, of course,' he muttered. 'Should have given that to you earlier.' He was too preoccupied to ask why I needed it.

I ran to the chest, which was in his cabin, and returned with it to George. I had been gone from him barely five minutes, but it seemed much longer. George was still white as a sheet, and had been sick right next to where he was slumped. He was still obediently holding his injured arm above his head, resting it on the side of the hull. He was more composed now, and looked quite bashful. Before, he had always acted the brave, big brother to me, but now I could see that he was ashamed of the way he had behaved.

He looked me in the eye, and said tersely, 'You won't tell anyone about the whimpering, will you?'

Anybody hit by a large wooden splinter would have made such a noise. I laughed, 'Of course not! Now let me get this splinter out.' I cut away the clothes around the wound, which were now quite bloody, but not soaked. I could see that George had been lucky with his injury – and it had not severed any major blood vessel. 'I'm going to pull it out, so hold tight . . .'

I held the end of the splinter carefully, and pulled slowly and firmly, taking care that none of it break off inside George's arm. He shut his eyes, making muffled shrieks between tightly clenched jaws. The splinter came out and I washed his arm with water. In the chest was a jar of 'Balm of Gideon' – a creamy ointment which I understood to be a healing lotion. It smelt so strongly it made my eyes water, and caught in the back of my throat. It stung the small cuts and abrasions on my fingers, just putting it on, so I could imagine how much it burned an open flesh wound. George's muffled shrieks grew more intense. Then I bandaged up the wound, helped George to his bunk, and went back on deck.

The sky had grown darker. The wind picked up, and a chill drizzle began to fall. I could see at once that the *Isabelle* had recovered from our initial lucky shot. She was still following us determinedly, although gaining on us at a slightly slower pace.

I tried to put a brave face on it, and turned to Filip Anders. 'At least she's not fired at us again,' I said.

He shook his head. 'That's not good news at all. Her captain's so confident in catching us, he's probably ordered his men to fire no more gun shots. These pirates are determined to take us as a prize. They don't want to damage their booty.'

Before Anders could say any more, Rushford shouted for us all to gather around him. 'The Frenchman is getting closer,' he said. 'Soon she'll be peppering our decks with musket and pistol shot. It's time to take up our own small arms and prepare to repel boarders. And remember, those of you with cutlasses, never raise them above your head to cut down a man. Any skilled and nimble opponent knows that this is the best time to strike. Keep your defence up at all times.

'Mr Clay. You and your gun crew are to load with

grapeshot, then move the gun to the starboard side of the quarterdeck. When the *Isabelle* comes alongside you are to fire across the length of the ship, just as her crew prepare to board us. The rest of you are to take up positions along the rail, and conceal yourself as well as you are able. Finally, I need two of you to go to the top of each mast, to fire down on the enemy.' He looked around the crew and his eyes alighted on me. 'You go to the foremast, Sam,' said Rushford. 'Keep yourself well hidden, lad, or they'll pick you off like a sparrow on a garden wall. And don't fire unless you're certain of hitting someone.'

The Captain had never called me by my first name before, and at first I was comforted by this unexpected show of affection. Then I realised he had spoken to me like that because he felt in his bones that we were minutes away from death.

We went at once to the ship's armoury. Two loaded pistols were placed in my hands, weapons which I had fired perhaps twice before in my life, and certainly never in anger. I was also presented with a cutlass, a weapon which I had never even held before. Then, with our sails between me and the Frenchman, I hurried to the top of the mast, doing my best to keep from view. Peeping out from between the sails I could see that the *Isabelle* was nearly upon us. On her deck I counted thirty men at least, crouching under cover from our occasional musket shots, and with their grappling hooks at the ready. We were outnumbered at least two to one.

On our deck I could see Clay and his gun crew hiding by their gun, ready to unleash a lethal shot. This at least might even the odds a little. I was surprised that I did not feel more frightened – after all, our enemy had made it plain she would take no prisoners. But when fear rose in my chest I glanced over to the shore at St Alban's Head and told myself that we were only five miles away from land. If the ship were overrun I could leap down from the mast and into the sea, and swim to safety. When other, more doubtful, thoughts entered my head, I shooed them away. I had to believe I was going to survive this battle . . .

The *Isabelle* drew closer, and lead shot began to thud into the side of our ship with some regularity. As she placed herself alongside she fired a single shot at our own gun, which was poking out at an angle from the stern. The ball hit home with an ugly splintering. In an instant it knocked the heavy gun over, then bounced up to take Mr Clay's head clean off his shoulders. As his lifeless body fell on its knees, I shut my eyes tight with horror, and swallowed hard to rid my mouth of the bile that had risen to the back of my throat.

The direct hit brought a cheer from the French ship, and then a further volley of musket and pistol shots. When I looked again I could see the two other men in our gun crew shrieking and writhing in agony, one crushed by the weight of the gun, the other peppered with splinters.

Just at that moment the sun came out. Almost immediately I heard a shot tear through the rigging of the mainmast behind me. I looked round and saw sunlight falling directly on the sails, silhouetting a shipmate named William Elliot, who was hidden behind the main topsail. Another shot rang out from the *Isabelle*. William screamed and fell. He hit the deck with a dull crump, dead twice over. Then a bullet punched a small hole in the sail next to my head, and I realised with skin-prickling horror that I must be just as conspicuous. Should I jump into the sea while I still had a chance? Or should I wait for the bullet that would surely knock me off my perch and have me fall to my death?

As stifling panic began to grip, I became aware of a voice shouting up to me. It was Captain Rushford.

'Sam! Sam! Come down quickly before you are shot!'

I didn't need telling twice and leaped at once for the rigging that would take me down to the deck. As I climbed down, shots whistled through the canvas but were all wide of their mark. When I reached the deck I realised I would have to stand and fight here. The *Isabelle* was now so close, any of us who raised a head above the rail risked a bullet in the brain. I crouched down on the deck behind the ship's cutter, next to the Captain, waiting to rush out at the oncoming boarders. I fumbled clumsily for my cutlass, but in my haste I brushed the sharp blade across the back of my hand, drawing blood.

The shadow of the French ship moved over us like a huge bird of prey. Shots were landing almost vertically on the planks close to our feet, as men high in the *Isabelle*'s masts fired straight down on to the deck. 'To the last, lad,' Rushford said to me, gripping my shoulder. Perhaps I should have been terrified, but now I was so fired up I felt like a coiled spring ready to tangle with anyone who came at me. There we waited, for the grinding jolt of ship crashing against ship, and the clang of grappling hooks curling over to embed themselves on our deck.

Instead we heard a desperate cry. 'Ennemi vaisseau, tribord!' I looked at Rushford, who understood immediately what was being said.

'It's a Navy ship!' he cackled, his face lighting up with relief. 'It's the Royal Navy come to rescue us. Keep down, Sam. We're not done yet,' he said quickly. He filled his lungs and shouted out, 'Hold fast, men. Stay under cover.' The shadow of the *Isabelle* moved away from us. Only after a couple of minutes did we feel safe enough to peer out from our sheltered positions. Sure enough, the *Isabelle* was now stern on to us. Sailing towards us from the coast was a handsome Navy warship, its white ensign fluttering fiercely in the breeze.

The Captain's eyes sparkled with delight. 'Ship of the Line. Must be a 74. She'll be able to chase off the Frenchman.'

Elated, I rushed below deck to tell George we were safe. But he turned away, his eyes refusing to meet mine. I suppose he felt he'd lost face in front of me when he had been wounded, and I was saddened because I had come to think of him as a friend.

The joy I felt on surviving the attack drained away like air from a balloon. Wearily I returned to the deck, to join the crew in the melancholy task of gathering together the dead. I had seen dead people before – the tiny, pockmarked corpses of my younger brothers, grandparents as shrunken husks in their coffins, and a pale drowned boy dragged from the river – but never men killed violently in battle.

We lost four men in the attack – Clay the most prominent among them. Also dead was Langan McKenzie, who had been one of Clay's gun crew. William Elliot, who fell from the mast, was an east countryman like me. He had been at sea for nearly twenty years. In truth, he was a stranger – I'd expected us to have something in common because we both came from the same county, but he always kept himself to himself. I looked at him now, and thought how easily it could have been me, lying cold and still, flecks of blood around my mouth, dead eyes staring up at the blustery sky. All of a sudden I felt very cold, and I ran below to fetch my jacket.

CHAPTER 2

Pressed

The Captain decided to bury the dead men as soon as possible. It was six o'clock, and we still had at least another two and a half hours of daylight. He ordered me to go below with Filip Anders to fetch four blankets from the dead men's bunks. Pulling a blanket away from the mattress I could not help but think that a man now to be consigned to the chilly depths of the sea had lain there that morning, safe and warm in the same grimy cloth.

We sewed the bodies inside the blankets, with a cannonball at their feet to make sure they sank. The Captain read the service so beautifully I thought he would have made a good parson. For the reading, he chose Psalm 103.

> *As for man, his days are as grass;*
> *as a flower of the field, so he flourisheth.*
> *For the wind passeth over it, and it is gone;*
> *and the place thereof shall know it no more.*

Rushford spoke movingly of Jeremiah Clay. 'He was a fine British seaman down to his boots and bones. I have to acknowledge that without Mr Clay's brave actions today, we would now almost certainly be heading for a grim and possibly fatal stay in a French prison.'

The Captain omitted to mention that thanks to him we could all have been killed, but it is easy to forgive the dead. Then, the ceremony over, all four men in turn were slipped into the sea, on a platform set up on the side of the ship. I did not relish the thought of a sea burial. The bottom of the sea must be a bleak and lonely resting place.

As the sun began to set we noticed that the Navy ship was still shadowing us, keeping a half mile or so to our stern. 'Perhaps she means to board us,' said Filip Anders, 'and press some of us into service.'

'Surely not,' I said, 'after what we've just had to suffer!'

Filip looked at me sharply and said, 'You've a lot to learn of this world, Master Witchall.'

As the remaining crew sat around the mess table that night, talk turned at once to the Navy ship. My ship-mates sometimes talked of the Royal Navy and most of them had a deep loathing for it. In their past, some of the crew had volunteered for the service, and others had been forced to join – 'pressed', they called it.

'Be warned, lads, especially when you're a few years older,' said one old salt to George and me. 'The Navy can board a merchantman and press who they like. It's the law, and there's nothing we or the Captain can do about it.

'Life on a fighting ship's a hair-raising business,' he went on. 'The bosuns beat their men with a rope to make them work faster. Y' wouldn't get that on the old *Franklyn*. Rushford knows he'd never be able to hire a crew if word got round that he was acting like that. But in the Royal Navy, if you complain you're looking at a flogging or hanging.'

George wasn't having this. 'No,' he jeered. 'Come on, that's traitor's talk. The British are a free-born race. The officers wouldn't permit such tyrannous behaviour.'

Even I looked sceptical at that last observation. By then our conversation had sparked the attention of Silas Warandel, a tall, wiry Londoner with a weather-beaten complexion, who wore his straw-coloured hair in a ponytail. Silas was something of a character on the *Franklyn* and I was curious to know what he had to say.

He strolled purposely over, placed his tattooed hands firmly down on the table, and leaned over to look George straight in the face.

'You, sunshine, obviously don't know your arse from your elbow. I joined the Navy as a ship's boy, like you. It was the worst decision I ever made in my life. Men on a fighting ship stay at sea for years on end. Their captains won't let them go on shore because they know that half the crew would desert. The food is ten times worse than the muck we get on this old bucket . . . meat and biscuits full of maggots.' He paused. 'You get used to the cold, bitter taste of 'em.'

Then he took off his shirt, revealing a back that was badly scarred. 'That, young man, is what happens to boys who join the Navy.' Silas was still aggrieved about his injury. 'I was flogged twenty times for having cross words with an officer. I cannot begin to tell you how horrible it is to be flogged, and if you join the Navy, my boy, you will be flogged as sure as day follows night. Each blow felt like a knife straight through my body. The pain shot like lightning to the tips of my toes and fingernails. As the flogging went on, I was sure that my lungs and organs would burst. When I passed out, they waited until I recovered my senses, and then they carried on. By the time they'd finished, my back looked like a piece of raw meat.'

We listened in a stunned silence, no one daring to speak. Silas carried on with his bleak warning. 'There is no justice or injustice in the Royal Navy,' he said, 'only duty and mutiny. All that you are asked to do is duty. All that you refuse to do is mutiny. And mutiny is punished by the whip or the noose. And there's many a man that's been flogged will tell you the noose is more merciful.'

With that, he turned his back on us and returned to his corner.

I was annoyed with George for provoking this response from Silas. He was quite a formidable character, and not a good man to cross. But although I was frightened of him, I was also intrigued. As I got to know the crew I discovered that he was a gifted seaman, but he could barely read or write. He also liked to drink, and when he drank his behaviour was the stuff of many a scandalous story.

Seven days after I first went to sea with the *Franklyn*, Silas had refused to get out of his bunk to take the Sunday morning watch, after a Saturday night nursing a bottle of rum. Captain Rushford, who had taken the previous watch despite having a high fever, reacted with uncharacteristic anger. When told of Silas's refusal to get out of bed, the Captain stormed over to his bunk in a rage. On the way down he had picked up a small bucket of sea water which one of the crew was using to clean the deck, and flung it over Silas. I heard him shout, 'Damn your bones, Mr Warandel. Get out of bed now, before I have you tied to the mainmast and flogged.'

Silas roused himself like an angry ferret from his bolt hole, and staggered to his feet. He took a swing at the Captain, missed pathetically, and ran out on deck.

'I'll see you drowned before you flog me,' he snarled, then ran to the rigging and scurried up to the very top of the mast.

Rushford, his anger spent, stared up at Silas, a dark blot against the dawn sky. 'Mr Warandel,' he cried in a voice which was attempting to sound conciliatory, 'come down at once, and let us put an end to this unseemly debate.' Silas, obviously unsettled by his exertions, leaned over the mast and retched noisily. The Captain stepped aside just in time, as a pool of vomit splattered down on the spot where he had been standing.

Silas stayed at the top of the mast for the rest of the morning. Whenever the Captain came out of his cabin, Silas would hurl abuse of the most hair-raising variety. Rushford simply pretended not to hear. When we were nearby the Captain, George and I tried not to catch each other's eye – we would have had a fit of uncontrollable giggling.

Silas came down just before noon and went at once to Rushford's cabin. What was said no one knew, but no more was heard about the incident. While the two men talked, Filip Anders told me they had sailed together for many years.

'Silas has the homing instinct of a seabird,' he said. 'He'll sniff the air, and know which way the ship should be heading. His feel for currents and tides comes from a lifetime at sea, not a year or two at a school of navigation.'

Filip had a high regard for Silas. 'Last year, when we were making slow progress close to the coast, I saw him pluck a feather from a chicken the cook was preparing for dinner, then toss it into the sea. He watched it float off, then warned the captain of dangerous currents to the lee of the boat. He saved us from certain disaster.'

Silas was more than a sailor, Anders told me; he was a carpenter, sail-maker, gunner, and helmsman too. On one Atlantic crossing, Anders said, the bow sprung a nasty leak in rough weather. Silas patched it up with a large piece of salt pork, a few nails and three small joists. It lasted the ship out until they returned home.

I slept badly that night, not least because of the dire warning Silas had given us about life in the Royal Navy.

When I tried to rest, I saw in my mind's eye the dreadful sights I'd witnessed during the day – the hull disintegrating before my eyes, William Elliot's fall from the mast, the violent death of Mr Clay and his gun crew – and I relived the moment the shadow of the *Isabelle* fell over our ship. While it was happening, I was too excited to think about it. But now, in the still, small hours of the night, I realised that I had probably been seconds away from death. A horrible, agonising death too – run through with a cutlass or a dagger, then pitched over the side still half alive, with not even a Christian burial to see me off. When I did fall asleep I would wake with a start, tormented by dreams. I fell into a deeper slumber only shortly before I was roused to take the early watch.

Out on the chilly deck, the sun was still two hours away from rising. Captain Rushford stood by the wheel. He was in remarkably good humour, but then he had much to be happy about. By a single twist of fate he had escaped with his ship and his life.

When I had set the sails as instructed, the Captain called me over to the wheel. He was joined by Filip Anders.

'Witchall,' said Rushford, 'Mr Anders is concerned that our friend over there,' he pointed to the distant lights of the Navy ship, 'is going to board us and press some of the crew. Now I'm sure they'll not press a boy as young as you, but I don't want to take any chances. If they come on board, go and hide yourself in the hold.'

I thanked the Captain, but began to feel a deep unease.

The Navy warship was still behind us when the day broke just after six o'clock, but she was edging closer. A little later I brought George some breakfast. He had been told to rest for a day, and so I sat down with him to eat. He seemed a little more friendly towards me, but was unconcerned by the news that we were being shadowed.

'It's of no consequence to me,' he said rather smugly. 'As I'm apprenticed, I'm exempt from the attentions of the Navy.'

'But what about me?' I said, feeling rather hurt.

'Well, Sam. The Navy needs men, and you'll be a fine one, I'm sure.'

I wish I'd had the wit to make some cutting reply, but in truth I was stunned by his callousness, and could think of nothing to say. I knew at once our friendship was over.

That morning I set about my usual tasks, cleaning the deck and trimming the sails. But my mind was not on my job. I kept thinking of the Navy ship to our stern, and wondered when they would choose their moment to come on board. But the trouble I feared actually came from another quarter. Just before ten o'clock that morning, when I was at the end of my watch and desperate to sleep, we were approached by another, smaller vessel on our larboard side, flying a large Navy ensign.

'She looks like a pressing tender to me,' said the Captain. 'She's probably already full of men seized by the press gangs. Must be heading for Portsmouth.'

'I'm sure she means to board us,' said Mr Anders.

'No matter,' said Rushford. 'We shall carry on and see what happens.'

The *Franklyn* sailed on. I flinched when I heard a gun shot. A plume of water erupted in the water ahead of our bows. They were telling us to heave to.

All hands were called on deck to bring the ship to a halt. As I ran up the masts to do this, I felt as though I was being told to dig my own grave. I knew the Navy ship would be watching, and they would spot me among the crew. There was nothing I could do. When the ship's sails had been taken in, I noticed a boat being launched from the tender, set to board us. I immediately ran to the Captain and asked if I could hide. 'Yes, lad, off you go,' he said. But he sounded so downhearted, I supposed that he already suspected they would take me.

As I ran below I saw Silas. He was looking agitated. 'I'm not going back to that. They'll not take me alive,' he said as I passed him.

'They'll not take you alive or dead,' said another seaman, but his joke fell rather flat.

I went at once to the hold, but it was almost bare – we

41

had emptied it trying to pick up speed to escape the *Isabelle*. I began to panic, realising I had only minutes before the Navy men would board our ship. Then I remembered a large locker in the forecastle near to my bunk, used for storing canvas sheets for sail repairs. I ran there at once, past George who seemed to be sleeping, and pulled out a large piece of canvas. I placed it untidily under the blanket of my bed, and squeezed into the locker as best as I could. Then I waited . . .

At first I could only hear my own breathing, and even fancied I could hear my heart, it was thumping so hard in my chest. I heard the dull clatter of a boat pressed hard against our hull, and the sound of feet scurrying aboard. There were muffled but agitated voices, and then Captain Rushford calling for all hands to assemble. With four of us dead and two of us down in the forecastle, the nine men standing before the press gang must have looked suspiciously few in number.

I heard raised voices and the sound of a struggle. I thought at once of Silas, and wondered if they had picked him. He, more than any of the surviving crew, looked every inch the hardened sea dog. Then there was a clatter of feet rattling down the ladder, and I peered through a small crack in the door to see who was coming.

Leading them down was a young man in a blue coat with brass buttons, white breeches and a cocked hat. A sheathed sword swung at his waist. He looked immaculately smart, and I recognised his uniform as that of a Navy lieutenant. He must have been sent along to accompany the crew of the pressing tender. His face was refined but sharp, and he wore a determined expression that declared him open to neither argument nor reason. With him were four burly thugs. They were not wearing any recognisable uniform and all of them carried wooden clubs. One time in Norwich I had seen the local hangman whip a felon through the streets. Each looked as villainous as the other, and if they had changed places no one would have been surprised in the least. Those men obviously had brothers, and here they were now.

They went at once to George. 'There you are, my fine fellow,' said the Lieutenant, with just a hint of mockery. 'Was that you we saw in the rigging?'

George seemed unruffled by their attention, until they made it plain they intended to take him off immediately. Then fear crept into his voice.

'I have documents, sir,' he cried, trying to sound important. 'I am apprentice to the Captain.'

The Lieutenant looked incredulous, and his cronies all laughed. 'I've heard that a few times, I can tell you,' he said. George raised himself from his bed, revealing his bandaged left arm, and plucked a key from a chain around his neck. With his good right hand he pulled a heavy chest from under his bunk, unlocked it, fetched out a plain envelope and handed it over.

The Lieutenant cast a brief eye over it, and tossed it back on the bed. 'You're obviously not the ragamuffin we saw in the rigging. Any idea where he might be?'

I held my breath and somehow I knew what would happen next. George didn't say anything. He just glanced over to the locker, lowered his head slightly and raised his eyebrows. I cursed myself for finding such a poor hiding place, but I was still white with anger that George had so readily betrayed me. Two of the men strolled leisurely over. The door creaked open and I froze as the light fell on me, feeling entirely naked and foolish.

'Come here, you,' said the Lieutenant. 'Was that you climbing the mast?' I stared at him, too furious to speak. He placed a hand on my arm and pulled me out of the cupboard. 'Up you go.'

Out on the deck, our crew were still standing before the rest of the party from the pressing tender – three other men and another officer. Also on board were three marines. I recognised them at once in their bright red coats. Silas was lying on the deck, with one of the gang standing over him. At first I wondered if he were dead, but then I saw he was breathing hard and his eyes were open, darting to and fro. He looked very, very angry.

'Just the two, I think, Mr Collinge,' said the

Lieutenant. Then he went to talk to Captain Rushford.

The other officer came over to me and said, 'Fetch your belongings, lad. If you can write, you've got ten minutes to pen a letter to your mother telling her what's happened.' Then he walked over to Silas, and prodded him with his polished black boot. 'You go and fetch your belongings too, and if there's any more trouble out of you we'll club you unconscious.'

I had only a small bag of possessions – clothes, a few keepsakes from home – and they were quickly gathered. I was so flummoxed by this turn of events I could think of nothing to say to my parents other than the plain facts of what had happened.

I passed George Mansell and whispered, 'You weasel.' He didn't look the least bit ashamed. I was so vexed I grabbed his injured arm and twisted it, and he yelped in agony. Then, on deck, Silas and I were each presented with a document from Captain Rushford, guaranteeing our pay up until this day. I wondered bitterly why I felt grateful.

I gave the Captain my letter and he wished me well. It was a formal farewell and I supposed he had said good-bye to several ship's boys in these circumstances. Just before we left, the Lieutenant spoke to us both again.

'If you volunteer at this point, then you will be entitled to a five pound bounty. The Royal Navy makes this offer to all men who come aboard, regardless of whether they have been pressed or volunteered.'

This was a significant sum – maybe nine months' wages aboard the *Franklyn*. But I was so angry at being seized, I refused it. Silas did too, and looked at me with a fierce pride.

'Very well,' said the Lieutenant, and smiled in a way that suggested he cared not a jot what we chose to do with his offer.

Almost immediately I regretted not taking the money. After all, it made no difference to my fate.

Then we were manhandled off the *Franklyn* and into the boat, and pushed off towards the Navy tender. I knew a little of what awaited me, and what I knew was enough to make me feel very afraid.

As the boat rowed closer to the tender, I wondered if I should jump into the sea and try to swim for shore. But it looked a formidable distance, and it was a cold morning – the kind of late summer day when the sunshine feels tired, and a chill wind blows in to remind you that autumn is coming. Besides, I was sat facing a marine with a bayonet pointed right at my stomach. I would almost certainly be run through before my head hit the water. Silas had even less chance of escape with his hands tied behind his back.

As we approached the tender I could see that she was perhaps half the size of the *Franklyn*. About her upper deck there were several more red-coated marines, all of them carrying muskets with fixed bayonets.

We pulled up alongside, and Silas and I were told to climb aboard. A marine untied his hands, and up the boarding ladder we clambered, bayonets to greet us, bayonets to prod us on our way. There were only a few souls on deck, but I could hear the low murmur of a large number of men coming up from below – like a strange human hive. A ghastly stench rose up to greet us.

We were swiftly ushered below, to a ladder which led to a large holding pen in the bowels of the vessel. Peering down through a hatch I could see scores of upturned faces – the hold was crammed with the most desperate bunch of men I had ever seen. Silas and I made our way down the small ladder and tried to find a place to stand. Although it was a cold day, the hold felt unbearably airless and hot. There was straw on the floor, and among the forest of arms and legs I could make out the occasional overflowing bucket. The smell was vile. Along with the usual human waste were pools of vomit from seasick men. I felt sick myself, but managed to control the urge to empty my stomach. There must have been a hundred men in the hold – certainly not enough room for all of us to sit or lie down at the same time. Some had managed to slump against the wall and sleep. Others had passed out, for want of air, I imagined.

The hatch closed over our heads and Silas and I stood

staring at each other. By the look on his face I guessed he was as dumbfounded as me. At first nobody talked to us – everyone seemed wrapped up in his own little bubble of misery. I saw that there was a large barrel of water at one end of the hold, and pushed my way over to drink from it.

Then, after half an hour, the hatch opened again, and the same lieutenant who had picked me out from the crew of the *Franklyn* called down. 'I want four volunteers to come up, two at a time, with the buckets of waste.' Immediately there was a score of men raising their hands to be chosen, hoping for a moment of fresher air away from the hold. The Lieutenant announced we would be given a midday meal – ship's biscuits. Each man had to come up separately to be presented with his ration. The process took nearly two hours. The Lieutenant then called down again. 'Gentlemen,' he said with a quaint formality, 'we have a good wind behind us and intend to reach Portsmouth by this evening, so you will not have to wait in the hold for much longer.'

The news seemed to brighten everyone's mood, and Silas and I began to talk to some of the other prisoners near to us. From what I could gather, most of the men in the hold came from Weymouth, where the press gang had descended with a vengeance. But several, like Silas and me, had been lifted from merchant ships.

One fellow with thinning blond hair and several days'

growth of beard told us he and three of his companions had been returning from a French prison.

'Three years, we'd been held,' he told us with mounting anger. 'Caught by privateers in the Channel, we were, and left to starve in a stinking Froggy jail. Three years . . . then there was one o' them exchanges of prisoners. They get some of ours, we give back some of theirs. 'Bout bloody time too. But soon as we reached the coast, the bastard Royal Navy plucks us from our ship . . .' By the time he finished his sorry tale he was so angry he could barely speak.

We did reach Portsmouth that evening. Slowly, we went from Navy ship to Navy ship, gradually emptying our human cargo. There were ten of us left in the hold when Silas and I were called up along with the last of the men. We assembled on deck, shivering in the sunset, surrounded by around twenty marines all pointing their muskets and bayonets directly at us. The Lieutenant came up to address us.

'Well, my lucky lads – this will be your new home.' He turned and gestured expansively towards a sleek-looking man-o'-war, which we were fast approaching. 'This is the frigate *Miranda* – the bravest, deadliest ship in the Navy.'

I guessed from his speech that he was a serving officer aboard the *Miranda*. Perhaps us ten men remaining on the tender he had judged to be the best of the crop? I turned to look at the ship, its three tall masts and rigging stark against the fading sky. In size she was perhaps twice the length of the *Franklyn*, and stood taller in the water.

She looked both elegant and lethal. From what I had been told, I knew that frigates were lightly armed – there was only one gun deck – but they were fast. 'The greyhounds of the sea', the *Franklyn*'s crew had called them. I also knew that of all the Navy ships, frigates were the most likely to be involved in action. At that moment I understood that whatever terrors I had been through the previous day with the *Isabelle* would be nothing compared to what I would have to face on the *Miranda*.

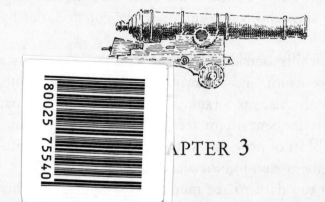

CHAPTER 3

His Majesty's Ship *Miranda*

As we grew nearer the *Miranda* I began to see her more clearly, and could now make out the ship's figurehead – a magnificent, bare-shouldered, buxom woman, with flowing white robes and long golden hair. A few dark shapes scurried around on deck. I felt tense and wary, and a painful knot had lodged in my gut. Silas was standing next to me and he spoke softly.

'I've been on one of these, my lad, and a frigate is a dangerous place to be.'

One of the marines hissed at him to shut up – and pointed his bayonet close to Silas's stomach. Shortly after, we bumped alongside the *Miranda*'s gangway. It was so small only a child could enter without stooping. We were shoved through and on to the gun deck one by one.

It was chilly outside, but inside the ship there was a clammy warmth, and a sharp tang of tar and creosote. Mixed with this was a rank, stale dishcloth odour that seemed to rise beneath my feet. I sensed it like an animal senses a beast of prey. It was the sort of smell that drifted from the prison in Norwich.

It was too dark to see much of the gun deck, other than a long row of guns receding into the gloom at either end of the ship. As we stood there, I heard a lone voice singing to a violin.

Red and rosy were her cheeks,
And yellow was her hair,
And costly were the robes of gold
My Irish girl did wear.

We were taken quickly below to the crowded mess deck, where there was no natural light, just one or two lanterns and a stifling fug. Faces turned round in sudden silence to look at us new arrivals. The dim lights cast murky shadows over their features, giving them something of the look of Hallowe'en ghouls. Then we were hustled even further below, to the hold.

Here too only a few lanterns lit the way. We were now below the waterline, in the belly of the ship. All around, piled high, were boxes, ropes and barrels. Rancid bilge-water, tar and hemp mingled to make an intimidating stench. The ship reeked of fear and brutality.

'Gentlemen,' said the Lieutenant, who had followed us all the way from the *Franklyn*, 'perhaps you'd be good enough to wait here while we go though the formalities.'

I found his mock courtesy irritating. Silas did too and said, 'Perhaps you'd be good enough to provide us all with a nice cup of tea. Only the best china cups, mind.'

All at once a thick-set thug, standing in the shadows behind us, stepped forward and delivered a hefty thwack to Silas's back with a knotted rope.

'Perhaps you'd be good enough to shut your face,' said the man in a matter-of-fact way – all the more effective for its calm authority. I noticed he wore a tall black hat with the ship's name painted on it.

The Lieutenant seemed completely unaffected by this act of unexpected violence. 'Meet Mr Tuck,' he said to us. 'He's one of the *Miranda*'s bosun's mates. He's here to keep an eye on you all. Now, I'm going to ask you to wait here while we enter your names into the ship's muster book.' He turned and vaulted up the stairs.

We crouched down on the floor and were called up two at a time. Even in the dim light I could see that the hold was spotlessly clean, like the rest of the ship. Silas began to tell me what to expect, but another blow from the knotted rope cut short our exchange. Eventually the two of us were marched up to the mess deck. Again, all conversation stopped. The entire deck was watching. Here we waited to be called further up. A few men continued to stare unashamedly, especially at me. Some were the cold, intimidating stares of bullies and thugs. Others were more leery – the kind of faces I had noticed on men staring at young women. I thought of a picture I had seen in one of my father's books of a lone antelope wandering the plains of Africa, being eyed up by a pack of lions.

'Don't show them you're frightened, lad,' whispered Silas, risking another clout from the rope. This time none came. Instead, the marines gave me an encouraging smile.

'You stare back and show them you're made of stern stuff,' said one.

I breathed deeply, and tried to feel angry rather than afraid. Now my eyes had grown accustomed to the light, I could take a proper look at the men I would be sailing with. The *Franklyn*'s crew numbered barely fifteen or twenty men. Here there were hundreds. Most I judged to be in their twenties – hardened sea dogs like Silas, brown and weather-beaten, tough as leather. There were a few older men too, and a scattering of youths and boys like me. The crew were a mixture of races too, with some darker faces, and a few black ones. Some carried the disfigurements of war – patches covering empty eye sockets, scarred arms and faces, missing fingers, even one or two missing legs . . . Some had tattoos – here a fiery sun or green mermaid, there a red dragon. One man, who wore only breeches, had a large and gory depiction of the crucifixion across his broad back. Underneath, close to his hips, were the words 'The Lord is a man of war'. I sensed he was not a good fellow to annoy.

I stood there aghast, wondering how I would survive with this brutal crew, and my eyes darted to and fro searching for a means of escape. Whatever happened, I was going to get away. Then a terse order came from above. A marine shoved me in the back to usher me upstairs. Silas was left below. There on the almost deserted gun deck, under the glow of a couple of lanterns, was a table at which sat the Lieutenant and another man. Now I was used to the gloom I could see the deck more clearly. Hefty beams crossed over a low ceiling that most grown men would have to stoop to navigate. The rows of red- and black-painted guns stood lurking by the gun ports on either side, catching some of the faint light of the lanterns. For a brief second I could imagine the noise and terror played out here when the *Miranda* went into battle.

'Good evening,' said the Lieutenant, in his cheery way. 'I am Lieutenant Middlewych, first officer on the *Miranda*. This is the ship's surgeon Dr Claybourne. We're going to ask you several questions about yourself, and make sure you're in suitably good health to serve aboard one of His Majesty's ships.'

Anger rose in my chest. I'd been dragged here against my will, and now they were telling me I might not be good enough for them. But I knew it was wise to say nothing.

'Sit down, lad,' said Middlewych, beckoning to a stool in front of the table.

Middlewych wanted my details for the muster book – the ship's records. Where was I born? What age was I? How long had I been at sea? All these questions I answered truthfully, but then he asked my parents' names and where they lived. 'We'll need to know where to look for you if you run away,' he said. I gave the right names, but on an impulse I blurted out a fictitious address in Norwich – a house in Chantry Road – a street my father and I passed through on our trips to the town. I was certain I was going to escape, and I'd be damned if I was going to help them find me.

Then I was rated – Boy Second Class. 'Behave yourself and you'll move up a rate before too long,' smiled the Lieutenant.

The doctor spoke then. He was a stout man in early

middle age, with a broad Scottish accent. 'Remove all y' clothes and stand just here.' There followed an unpleasant minute of prodding and poking, while I stood naked and burning with humiliation. I felt like a horse being examined on market day. 'He's in good health,' said the doctor. 'No evidence of disease. Now go and wash in that bucket over there.'

I washed quickly, then they gave me some fresh clothes – canvas trousers, short jacket and chequered shirt, all too big. 'You can scrub your own clothes clean tomorrow,' said the Lieutenant, 'and use these as a second set. The cost will be deducted from your wages. Now wait below, and we'll find you a berth.' I heard him call over a marine, and order him to find someone or other.

By now it was late in the evening and I was sick and dizzy with exhaustion. A tall, stocky man with a bald head came up to me. He looked around my father's age.

'Crikey – they've sent us a babee!' he said. 'Next thing we know, we'll be getting wenches to work with!'

I looked at him with baffled irritation. He ignored my ill manners and smiled, then put out a hand for me to shake.

'So you're Sam, aren't you? Bad luck, lad, getting yerself landed in this blasted palaver. My name's Ben Lovett. Lieutenant Middlewych tells me I'm to be your Sea Daddy. D'you know what that is?'

I shook my head. I was so wrapped up in my own misery, I could barely bring myself to speak.

'I'm to look after you while you get to know the ship,' he went on. 'I'll be telling you what to do and how to carry out your duties. Where to sleep, where to eat, where to take a leak . . . Come and sit down and we'll have a chat.'

Ben had a friendly face and I liked him immediately. His accent was one I didn't recognise, so I asked him where he was from.

'I'm from Birmingham, me,' he said. 'Not many sailors from Birmingham. It's all foundries, coal mines and canals.' He stopped and sighed. 'Lord knows how I ended up goin' to sea. Should have gone on a canal boat. Y' don't get many storms in a canal. Or French frigates, for that matter.

'Did you take the bounty?' he asked. By now I felt quite stupid for not taking the five pounds I had been offered, and was embarrassed to tell him I didn't. But he whispered, 'Good for you. I didn't take it either, when they got me. Just because they've got your body doesn't mean you have to sell them your soul! I think we're going to get on, you and me.'

His unexpected kindness in this frightening world almost brought me to tears. He noticed, and spoke to me sternly. 'C'mon now, Sam. We'll have none o' that crying. This is not a good place for tears.'

Ben took me to the steward's room, where I was issued with two hammocks and a blanket. I had to pay for the blanket too – thirteen shillings to be taken from my wages. By now most of the ship was asleep, and we picked our way through a forest of sleeping men on the mess deck, to a space near the bow.

'I'm not going to show you how to do this now,' whispered Ben. 'I'll show you when there's more light and you're not so tired.' He swiftly undid the ropes that tied my hammock together, and slung it on hooks between two beams. 'I'll show you gettin' in tomorrow, as well,' he said with a wink, and quickly lifted me under the armpits, and swung me into the hammock. I had never been in a hammock before. On the *Franklyn* we had slept in wooden bunks. The hammock felt comfortable and even quite snug, when I had wrapped the blankets around me. Ben slung his hammock next to mine. Right leg up, left hand holding the top, a jump up, twist round, and he was in.

I was so tired I could have slept on a marble floor. But barely had my head touched the pillow, it seemed, than I woke next morning with a bosun's mate howling 'Out or down' in my ear. I sat straight upright in surprise and lost my balance, plummeting to the deck. Tears sprang to my eyes, and Ben came swiftly to my aid.

'Quick, now,' he said. 'In the morning you need to get

out of that hammock at double speed. Stay in there and they'll cut you down. Now, watch this . . .' With that, he rolled up his hammock and bedding, and roped it tight together. I followed the best I could, but I was groggy with sleep and had a thick headache. 'Not bad, not bad,' said Ben, but undid the lot and did it again himself. 'Now come and eat your breakfast.'

Ben beckoned me to sit down with him at one of the long wooden tables on the mess deck. As we began to eat our oatmeal we were joined by his friend Colm, an Irishman who had been pressed three years ago. He made no secret of his dislike of the Royal Navy, but he told me, 'We all have our cross to bear here on the *Miranda*. I reckon if I keep my head down and do as I'm told, I'll come out of this life in the Navy without being flogged or killed.'

There was something about Colm that made me trust him, so I told him and Ben I'd given Lieutenant Middlewych a false address for his muster book. I felt proud of my deception, and wanted to impress my new shipmates. But they weren't impressed.

'Aren't you the clever article, Sam,' scoffed Colm. 'How are you going to change that now? You could be flogged for it.'

My mouth went completely dry and I began to feel faint.

'Flogged?' I blurted out.

Ben butted in. 'Don't scare the lad, Colm. I doubt they'd flog him for that.'

'Maybe so,' Colm went on, 'but how're you going to write to your family without some sharp-eyed busy-body of an officer noticing the address is different from the one in the muster book?'

That was it. I had to get away as soon as I could. 'I'll be gone before that happens,' I said defiantly.

'Sam, you haven't got an ounce of sense in your bonce,' chided Ben. He obviously didn't take me seriously. 'I've never known a man get off this ship. They were killed trying, or ended up getting flogged or hung from a yardarm.'

I cursed myself for not keeping my own counsel. 'There's nothing to it then, I suppose. I'll just have to confess . . .' I said.

Ben spoke. 'No, mate. Just keep quiet for now and see what happens. Right now there's too many other things for you to worry about. When we're done here I've to take you to see the Captain. He's going to tell you what you're going to be doing.'

So after breakfast he led me up to the Captain's cabin. It took up the entire rear end of the gun deck, with a set of windows that ran over the width of the stern. Light streamed in, catching on silver candlesticks and polished mahogany. Lieutenant Middlewych was there, sat behind a table. Next to him was a slightly older man.

Judging by the lavish amount of gold braid around his hat and coat, and the immaculate look of his clothing, there was no doubt this was the Captain. He looked at me with something between a sneer and a smirk, his pointy nose wrinkling with distaste. Middlewych's manner was now quite different, too. He was sitting stiffly upright and greeted me with cold eyes, and no nod of recognition. I stood before them waiting for someone to speak, wishing I could sit down, not least to steady my trembling legs. Ben was curtly dismissed.

They waited for him to leave before either spoke. 'Good morning, Master Witchall,' said the Captain, in a brusque, well-spoken voice. 'I am Captain Mandeville. I understand you were pressed yesterday evening. You are now under Navy regulations, and subject to the full Articles of War. That, to be perfectly clear, means you can be flogged for neglect of duty, insubordination, drunkenness and anything else I think fit. If you desert, or strike an officer, you will be hung from the yardarm. Lovett will instruct you further in the Articles of War. I advise you most strongly to pay heed. Your friend Mr Warandel can tell you what it's like to be flogged, so try not to cross me.' He gave a beady, humourless smile, then continued. 'Lieutenant Middlewych here tells me you're nimble in the rigging. We may yet call upon your services in that area, but for the moment we've no need for topmen on the *Miranda*. What we need is a powder boy for the gun crews. The last boy we had failed to put the top on his powder canister when we attacked a French brig. A stray spark floated down and blew him to a pink mist. AND it made a dreadful mess of my ship. You look fast on your feet, so I'm sure you'll fit the bill.' Then he turned to the Lieutenant and nodded for him to continue.

Middlewych gave a nervous cough. 'You've been placed in the larboard watch,' he said, 'in the afterguard. Your duties will include pulling and hauling the sails and whatever else is demanded of you, but your chief concern will be gunnery. When called "To Quarters" you'll supply powder for the gun just aft of the larboard main hatch. Pay attention, learn your trade, and try not to get yourself blown up. You will join Lovett's crew, and he will train you in all these duties. He's a good, kind man –'

'A kind man?' interrupted the Captain. 'I've little use for kind men on this ship.'

Middlewych looked uncomfortable, and I almost felt sorry for him. He waited a moment, to see if the Captain had anything more to say. '. . . And I'm sure you won't disappoint him and us. That is all.'

This I took to be my signal to leave, and I nodded in what I hoped was a respectful manner. As I turned to go, the Captain called out, 'Witchall. Next time I see you, you'd better have learned how to salute.'

I spent the morning scrubbing out the hold with four

other newly pressed men. They were all much older than me and none seemed keen to talk. Whistles blew just after noon, and I turned to a ratty-looking man with ginger bristles on his chin and asked what this meant.

'That's the signal to go to the mess deck for dinner, lad,' he said as we trooped up the stairs. 'I've been in this pickle before. Y' life's ruled by that bosun's whistle – breakfast, dinner, hauling yourself up to the yards, weighing the anchor. You obey that whistle just as a soldier obeys a bugle.'

I spotted Ben seated at a table in the corner and picked my way towards him, avoiding the curious stares of the older seamen.

'So – you're to be a powder monkey!' he said.

'Why do they call us that?' I said. It sounded insulting.

Ben laughed. 'Don't get on your high horse, Sam! Monkeys are nimble creatures. That's what you need to be, so that's what you ought to become.'

'And what's the afterguard?' I said.

'The afterguard's the division that's stationed on the quarterdeck – y' know, that bit at the stern where the Captain stands.'

I realised Ben liked to tease me by pretending I knew nothing about life at sea. He went on, 'The larboard watch take turns with the starboard watch. Your duties there probably won't be a great deal different from what you had to do on the *Franklyn* – cleaning the ship, operating the sails and the like.'

'What about climbing the rigging?' I asked anxiously.

'A bit o' that, for sure. But the topmen do most of that work.'

I was pleased I would not have to regularly climb the rigging. I felt confident up in the sails of the *Franklyn*, but the masts on the *Miranda* were much higher. I feared the letting down and furling of the sails would be done with a speed that took little account of safety.

'Your chief duty, though,' said Ben, 'is to assist in the firing of the guns.'

Ben took great pride in his work as a gunner. It was obvious the moment he spoke about it. 'The British gunner is the best in the world, Sam. That's why Britannia rules the waves!' I didn't doubt it. After all, I'd grown up hearing about the Royal Navy's famous victories. Ben went on, 'It's not the captains, it's not the ships, it's us that win the battles. We train and we train, until we can load and fire those guns blindfold – not that we've ever tried, mind, but we've sometimes had to fight at night. And when we fight we can get our guns to fire one shot a minute. The Frenchies and the Spanish can't do that to save their lives. We're twice as fast as they are. And that's why we're the best.'

Before the meal was over I remembered to ask Ben to

show me how to do a Navy salute.

'You need to salute with your right hand every time you see an officer,' he told me. 'And turn your palm away from the man you salute, so he can't see your mucky hands. You practise a few times. And don't forget, you can be flogged for insubordination if you don't salute.'

Ben took me up to the gun deck to look at the ship's guns. Daylight streamed in through the main gangways of the ship. Posted by each was a marine standing to attention in his bright red coat. On the starboard side, where the ship faced the quay, a gangplank led down to the harbour. I looked out, beyond the guard, to the quayside behind him. If I chose my moment, surely I could run past him?

Ben could read my thoughts, and spoke quietly. 'You'd be dead by the time you got halfway down the gangplank, Sam, if you hadn't been run through with a bayonet before you even got out the ship. There's a marine at every hatchway. And one by every mooring rope.

'You'll find the marines keep themselves well apart from the sailors. It's no wonder. They're supposed to keep order. And they're expected to kill any one of us who tries to escape.'

The marine standing guard sensed we were talking

about him. 'State your business,' he barked.

Ben gave him a quick smile. 'It's none of yours, my friend. I'm here to show our new powder monkey the guns.'

I wondered how many of his previous powder monkeys had heard this speech, but thought it wise not to ask.

'There's thirty-two big guns on this ship, which is why it's called a "32". There's ten either side of the gun deck, and another six either side of the forecastle and quarterdeck. I'm captain of the crew of this gun here, next to the larboard hatchway.'

Ben pointed to his gun.

'These big guns are called 18 pounders, because they fire 18lb shot.' He nodded towards a line of black metal cannonballs placed underneath the gun ports. I went to pick one up. It was slightly above the width of a man's hand, and almost more than I could lift.

'You try to move that gun,' he instructed. I placed my back against the wooden carriage and shoved with all my might. It didn't budge an inch. I may as well have been pushing at a huge tree trunk. 'These guns and carriages are nearly two tons apiece. We keep the guns loaded once we go out to sea, so they're ready to fire if we're attacked. Once the first broadside is fired, we need to reload as soon as possible. That's why your job is so important. Gunpowder's too dangerous to be kept by the guns, so you need to run to the magazine and fetch it. We're close to the magazine here, so you won't have far to run. I'll show you.'

We walked down the ladder nearest to Ben's gun, to the mess deck and then down another stairway which led to the after magazine. Here in the dark belly of the ship was one of the two chambers where gunpowder was kept. Another marine was standing guard beside it. Ben gave him a curt nod.

'This is where you come to fetch the gunpowder cartridges. They're made of linen bags and you carry them in a leather container, which we call a cartridge box. You make sure the lid's on good and proper, Sam, and you'll be all right.'

Even now, in port and far from battle, the magazine was an unsettling place to be. The few dim lanterns in the hold cast a faint glow, creating an atmosphere of demonic menace. Here, I supposed, there was enough gunpowder to blow the entire ship, and everyone on it, into fragments of wood, flesh and bone.

As the crew gathered in the mess for supper that evening I spotted Silas.

'What have they been making you do today, Mr Warandel?' I asked.

'Call me Silas, Sam. We're in this hornet's nest together. I've just spent four hours in the forecastle repairing the ship's rigging. I had a chat with that Mandeville this morning too. Have you met him yet?'

I nodded.

'Beady-eyed bastard. Tells me he's got his eye on me.'

I smiled, but could think of nothing useful to say. I was pleased to see Silas, but he made me feel uneasy and I wondered what he might do that would land me in trouble.

'I'm joining you in the larboard afterguard, Sam. I've been put in with Ben Lovett's gun crew. Have you met him yet? Can't say I care much for Brummies, especially that one. Being gun captain's probably the first bit of power he's had in his life, and he's keen to let everyone know he's the boss.'

I thought Silas sounded a little jealous. 'He's all right, is Ben. He's my Sea Daddy.'

Before I could say more, Ben came over to join us. He smiled at me, but gave Silas more of a curt nod. I sensed the two of them had not hit it off.

Ben took us over to a table where he usually sat. This time he introduced us to his mess mates.

'This is Silas Warandel. He's from London. And the lad here is Samuel Witchall. You're from Norfolk, aren't you? They'll be replacing Henry and Stephen.' The men all nodded indifferently.

Silas asked the question I had not dared to. 'What happened to Henry and Stephen?'

Ben shook his head. 'Horrible business. Henry was crushed by the gun. Stephen was blown to pieces by his cartridge box.'

There was a brief pause as some of the men took off their hats and whispered a silent prayer. Ben turned directly to us. 'You'll have to get used to this lot, Sam, and you too, Mr Warandel. They're my gun crew, and we all eat together every mealtime. You can see they're a fine cross section of the Royal Navy.'

We ate our bread and cheese as Ben carried on talking. 'In training and combat, we're all called by a number, rather than a name. I'm Number One, and you, Sam, are Number Twelve. My job's to oversee the loading and aiming of the gun, and fire the flintlock that sets it off. Then there's Tom Shepherd here.' He pointed to a solid, bespectacled young man. 'He's a Londoner and he's my Number Two. He cleans out the gun, then reloads it. After me, he's the most important man in the crew. If he does it wrong, the powder could explode whilst the gun's being loaded. It's a job for a steady man, and we all trust Tom to do it well.'

Tom smiled at me and leaned over to shake my hand. 'I was a merchant seaman like you, Sam,' he said. 'I sailed out of London. I was pressed on the way back from America. My old mum always told me to stay away from the sea.' He laughed. 'She was right! Crossed the Atlantic, didn't I, and ended up in this.'

Ben went round the table. 'This here's our Number Three, James Kettleby. He helps me aim the gun. Y' need to be as strong as an ox to do that job.'

James was certainly big and burly. He was from Newcastle, and his accent was hard for me to follow. Tom immediately began to rib him about the way he spoke. 'Are y' gannin doon toon the neet?' said Tom.

'Aye,' said James, with amiable contempt. 'Ah gannin doon toon t' find me a bonny lass. Captain's given me special leave like – t' get away from soft Cockney bastaads like ye!'

This exchange made me nervous. I couldn't understand how two men could talk to each other with such apparent hostility, but both be laughing when they spoke.

Ben went on, 'Four, Five and Six help to manhandle the gun. You know Silas – he's Number Four.' Ben continued around the table. 'Then we've Oliver Macintosh.' He nodded to a dark-skinned man. 'He's Number Five. Escaped a life of slavery in Jamaica to volunteer for a life of slavery in the Royal Navy. Can't say you notice much difference, eh, Oliver?'

Oliver raised a weary eyebrow and shrugged. 'Ahm a free man 'ere, as much as any o' you lot. An' I get paid the same money, so I'd say it were a better life, yes.'

This was a debate no one wanted to get drawn into, so Ben moved on to the final man in his crew. 'And this is

Edmund Ackersley from Bolton, Lancashire. He's Number Six. He's a volunteer as well.'

I couldn't understand why an ordinary seaman would volunteer for a life aboard a fighting ship, so I asked Edmund why he did it. He'd worked in a mill, he said, and had struggled to feed his growing family.

'By 'eck, I never had enough for nuthin'. Y' get more meat on a Navy ship than we ever 'ad at 'ome. Bit o' bacon once a week, and a few potatoes. Cheese I never 'ad till I came on board. I like the Navy life. Y' don't have to worry yerself about nowt, save gettin' killed or maimed o' course! No candles t' buy, no rent t' worry about, no wood f' fire. No moanin' missus and screamin' infants. It suits me fine.'

The other men round the table raised their eyes to the ceiling when Edmund talked. I sensed they did not care for his company. I could see why.

Edmund started to tell me about the boy I'd replaced, who'd been blown to pieces when a stray spark floated into his half-opened cartridge box. I quickly said that Captain Mandeville had already told me. That didn't stop him. 'Nothing left of him except his feet and the stumps of his ankles.' The men also told me about the powder monkey who'd had both his arms blown off when a lucky musket shot had hit his cartridge box. 'He looked like a seal after that,' said Edmund, with rather too much glee for my liking.

I didn't want to hear, but the more I protested, the more it spurred them on. 'One lad had his insides blown out at the top of the hatchway. Gizzards caught in the coaming, and when he fell down the stairs they all spooled out. It was horrible.' I got paler and paler. Only when they told me about the boy who'd been blown to pieces and all that was left of him were a pair of teeth and his eyeballs, and the teeth had said, 'My, that stings,' did I realise that they were teasing me.

I knew seamen often joked about the things they feared most, but this wasn't helping me at all. Sometime very soon, if I could not escape before we took to sea, I would have to help fire these fearsome weapons.

CHAPTER 4

The *Miranda* Goes to Sea

The *Miranda* stayed in Portsmouth for six more days. Having not put my feet on dry land for weeks, I longed to walk out of the ship on to the harbour, and then just keep walking, past the sentries, past the dockyard, past the confines of the town and all the way back home. But the more I became familiar with the ship and her routines, the more I understood I had no more chance of escaping than walking on the moon. I had not completely given up though. I reasoned that the best opportunity to escape would come when the ship sailed away from harbour – especially if I was asked to let down the sails.

We put to sea one early September morning. As I'd hoped, I was ordered up the rigging to set the mizzen topgallant. Ben stood next to me on the foot rope, ready to let fall the canvas. There at the top of the mast I was filled with a gnawing anxiety – both for what I hoped to do, and for what would happen if I did not succeed. I looked over to the town of Gosport on the far side of the harbour. A good, strong swimmer should be able to make that shore, if the current didn't defeat him. I had never swum such a distance before, but I felt it worth the risk. Then I looked down the mast. The deck seemed an almighty distance, the water even further. Could I survive a jump into the water?

The alternative – staying on the *Miranda* – made the risk worthwhile. I had to choose my moment carefully. A leap powerful enough to clear the rail and then I'd strike out for that far shore.

All around, in sharp autumn sunshine, were Navy ships. The city stretched out, chimneys smoking, spires pointing, streets bustling. In the distance, the trees in the woods outside the city were taking on a golden hue.

My thoughts were interrupted by Lieutenant Middlewych, shouting through his speaking trumpet. 'Trace out, let fall!' Down dropped the sails and the ship began at once to move away from the quay. This was it. My final chance to escape.

The bosun's whistle blew, the signal for those in the rigging to return to the deck. Instead, I began to edge out along the starboard yard, intending to get to the tip, where I would have the best chance of jumping clear. Ben knew at once what I was doing, and grabbed my arm.

'Sam,' he hissed, 'don't be stupid. They'll shoot you in the water.'

I pulled away, determined to go. But Ben would not let me. His grip tightened and he looked me in the eye and said calmly, 'If they have to send a boat out to get you, you'll be lucky if you only get flogged. Desertion is a hanging offence. Don't do it, Sam. You're throwing away your life.'

Then a bosun's mate shouted up from the deck. 'You men in the mizzen topgallant. Down at once!'

My determination to go ebbed away. What had I got myself into? We scuttled down, I with my heart in my mouth wondering what punishment I would face with my mad plan to escape.

Lieutenant Middlewych was waiting. 'Lovett, what on earth was going on up there?'

Ben was supremely confident. 'Lad lost his nerve, sir. He's not very good in the rigging.'

Middlewych was unimpressed. 'He looked good enough to me on that merchantman the other day.'

'I'm sorry, sir,' I said. 'I'm not used to being so high up. I promise it won't happen again.'

'Make sure it doesn't, lad,' he said.

Out of earshot of the Lieutenant, Ben was livid. 'Never, EVER, pull that trick on me again. If Middlewych had chosen not to believe me, we'd have both been flogged.'

Throughout the morning we sailed against the wind. It was past eleven o'clock before we were away from the city, heading down to the Solent. It took another day before we left the coast behind at Portland Bill. Mandeville called his crew together and informed us that we were to patrol the Bay of Biscay and Spanish coast, then stop off at Gibraltar to resupply. Our quarry would be any French or Spanish ship that crossed our path.

I took a long look at the distant cliffs, and wondered if this would be the last I'd see of England. In the other direction, where we were heading, lay a vast expanse of open sea. One side, safety. The other, danger. What would I give now, to trade this life for the humble chores of my uncle's shop?

Away from harbour, the *Miranda*'s daily routine changed considerably. Depending on the watch we took, on some nights we had only four hours' sleep. There were breaks in the afternoon or evening, when it was possible to catnap, but the ship was hardly filled with cosy sofas and armchairs. I was tormented by this constant lack of sleep, especially on the long dreary night watches either side of four a.m. While other sailors dreamed of fine food or women, I longed for a fresh warm bed, and the freedom to stay in it until the weariness had left my bones.

In some ways life aboard the *Miranda* was similar to that in the *Franklyn*, with its daily round of cleaning, mending and tending. But learning to live with so many people in such a small space was no pleasure at all. At night we bedded down in the mess deck, shoulder to shoulder in our hammocks. Despite the constant rumble of snoring, belching, farting, sleep-talking and nightmare groaning that surrounded me, I managed to sleep well enough. I was so exhausted at the end of each day I could have slept through the Great Fire of London. But I never got used to the waking up. At the sound of the bosun's shrill whistle we would be roused from a deep sleep and have to spring to our feet, lest our hammocks be cut down or our heads assaulted by a knotted rope.

After a night in such a crowded space, my head would ache and I had a foul, coppery taste in my mouth – as if I had slept with a penny under my tongue. I suppose this was due to lack of air.

As soon as we were up, we rolled our hammocks and placed them in netting at the side of the ship. The wooden beam below was marked by numbers apportioned to us, so we knew exactly where to place our hammock. I was 195. Having the hammocks packed like this was supposed to offer protection against musket balls and splinters. Then we relieved our bladders in the piss dales or at the heads in the bow of the ship. There were only two seats for all the two hundred and fifty ratings on board, so first thing in the morning men would lean up against the bow netting at the side of the ship where the wind blew away from them, and piss into the waves. If the sea was high and the wind blew hard the cold would cut like a knife. It was a brutal start to the day – especially after the warmth and fug of the mess deck – but it cleared your head of sleep.

I was outraged to discover that Captain Mandeville had two private closets to himself, on either side of his Great Cabin, to use as he chose, whichever way the wind was blowing against the ship. Even the officers on the frigate did not have their own closets, but at least they had cabins, chamber pots and servants. We ordinary sailors had none. At first I was embarrassed to sit on the head in the company of a small but impatient queue of other sailors in various states of desperation. Attached to the head was a long rope with a feathered end which dangled in the sea. When a man had finished moving his bowels, he would haul the rope up to clean himself. I tried not to think about everyone else using that same rope.

*　*　*

Once awake we hurried to the mess tables for breakfast. It was most often oatmeal porridge, which the men called 'burgoo' – but it was warm and filling, and set me up for the day ahead. We washed it down with 'Scotch Coffee', a piping hot drink made from burned biscuit crumbs and sugar. It took some getting used to, but kept the chill from my bones.

Always we would clean. I soon discovered why the *Miranda* looked so spotless. I wore my fingers raw scouring the deck with sand and a large sandstone block. The men called these 'holy stones' because they were the same size as a church Bible. Most days we practised our sail drill, but everyday we drilled on the guns. For the first few days at sea this was without shot and cartridge – just going through the motions. But on the first Friday away from Portsmouth, Ben told me we were to fire the guns for real. I tried to hide my fear, but my hands would not stop shaking.

The drummer boy began to beat 'To quarters' – our signal to go at once to our battle positions – and I ran as fast as I could to the after magazine. Inside were one of the gunner's mates and his assistant, who had stacks of paper cartridge bags filled with gunpowder in readiness for us. As I had been instructed I shouted 'Powder' and a hand passed the cartridge out to me. I grabbed it, put it in the cartridge box as fast as I could and jammed down the lid. Then I sprinted upstairs to my gun.

All in place around our gun, we stood ready to fire the first broadside. After the first shot from our gun we would have to reload and fire again as soon as we could. Utter silence settled on the ship as we awaited the command of one of the ship's lieutenants, Lieutenant Spencer.

'Larboard guns, fire!' yelled Spencer.

The noise was awe-inspiring. A thunderous roar made the ship shake from topgallant to keel. The gun in front of me recoiled on its ropes, lurching back like a wild animal trying to free itself from its shackles. My ears rang for several minutes afterwards. I understood that it was customary for gun crews to wear no shoes, as bare feet were supposed to offer better grip against the wooden deck. But seeing first hand how these heavy weapons sprang to life, I would have thought stout metal-capped boots would be more in order.

All ten guns fired on our larboard side, followed immediately after by nine on our starboard. Only one, opposite us, did not go off. Perhaps the powder was damp? I heard Lieutenant Spencer cursing, and the gun crew exerting themselves to shift the gun away from the gun port to extract the shot.

After that first broadside, we worked in a frenzy to reload and fire again as soon as possible. 'Extra grog for the crew who fires first, and extra scrubbing of the deck for the crew who fires last,' shouted Spencer.

Tom swiftly cleaned out the gun with a sponge on a pole, to make sure there were no glowing fragments from the previous cartridge. Then the new gunpowder cartridge was snatched from my hand and rammed down the barrel of the gun with the other end of the pole, swiftly followed by the cannonball – we called it the shot – then a wad of old canvas to keep it in place.

The others, led by James who carried a hand spike for the purpose, heaved the gun carriage back into position, so that the gun poked out of the gun port. It was back-breaking work.

Ben poked a wire down the touch hole by the flint-lock to pierce the cartridge. Then he carefully sprinkled more powder down the touch hole from a horn he carried on his belt, and pulled back the mechanism of the flintlock. He shouted out 'Make ready', warning us all to stand away, then fired the gun by pulling a cord to trigger the flintlock. The sparks lit the powder in the touch hole, and KERRRANG, the beast spat flame and smoke and lurched again on its harness.

Our team had worked hard to reload and fire first, but we were narrowly beaten by a gun crew over on the starboard side. Ben looked rattled by this failure, although he chose not to say anything to us all.

In those first few days at sea I built up a fierce resent-ment for the relentless drilling and cleaning. Life on the *Franklyn* had been much easier. I made the mistake of complaining to Ben. He huffed impatiently.

'This is all about staying alive, lad. First of all, when you're scrubbing and polishing just think about the two hundred and fifty men we've got on this ship. Can you imagine the stink and pestilence if we let the dirt build up? And as for drilling . . . when we come to fight, you'll be grateful for the hours you spent making sure you knew exactly what you're doing.'

Everything stopped for dinner – our main meal of the day. We would sit down just after the noon sighting, when the officer on duty took the daily navigational readings, to spend an hour and a half eating and talking.

Quickly I realised we had the same thing for every day of the week. Monday was cheese. Tuesday was beef. Wednesday was pease and cheese. I would have enjoyed some of it had I not cracked a back tooth on a bone aboard the *Franklyn*, and now it was nagging away every time I chewed on it.

All of our food was washed down with a pint of grog – a little rum in water. It wasn't enough to get a man drunk, just a bit happier. And it took away the horrible taste of the water, which would be all but undrinkable after we had been at sea for a month or more. The first time I took the grog it made me feel dizzy, but I soon got used to it, and even began to look forward to my daily dose.

In the afternoon we would drill and clean again.

Supper was at five o'clock. It was usually just ship's biscuits, which tasted like dry stale bread, and were usually crawling with maggots. And more grog.

'If we're lucky we might get some tea at some point, or cocoa,' said Ben.

I shrugged indifferently.

'Shrug if y' like, lad,' he chided. 'You'll be grateful for a change. And when it comes round it'll taste like nectar after what we usually drink.'

When we were not working there was little else to do but sit, drink and talk. Although drunkenness was punishable by flogging, most of the time the officers would pretend not to notice a man who was unsteady on his feet, or whose speech was slurred.

As the day wound down we would gather together in little clusters. The older seamen told tales, and we sat and listened. Some of these yarns became like favourite bedtime stories, and I was happy to hear them over and over. Some ten years previously, one of our crew, Tom Nisbit, had sailed with Captain Bligh on his *Bounty* expedition to take breadfruit plants from the Pacific to the West Indies. Nisbit was one of the eighteen men who stayed loyal to their captain when the crew mutinied. He told us excitedly how they had been cast adrift in the ship's launch, and that Bligh had sailed his remaining crew for fifty days through uncharted waters to reach the trading port of Kupang on Timor Island. Tom was obviously haunted by his ordeal. His mood lightened when he spoke fondly of his famously irascible captain.

'Without that man I'd be lying at the bottom of the Pacific Ocean, or had me bones picked clean by savages.' Having experienced starvation and near fatal thirst first-hand, Tom got annoyed when anyone moaned about their food. 'We ate raw seabird on that little boat – beak, feet and all. After that, a ship's biscuit looks like a king's feast!'

When we weren't talking, those of us who could, read or wrote. I was grateful to my father for teaching me these skills. Word soon went round the ship that I could write, and I was often asked by sailors who could not to help them with a letter. This was a good way of staying on the right side of some of the more frightening members of the crew. These letters were sometimes very personal – a plea to an estranged wife, or words of comfort to a sister or brother who had lost a child.

I learned quickly not to take too great a pride in my skill. I thought I was being generous with my time and talents, yet some of the crew started to resent me for it. As I wrote, older boys would walk past and flick my ear. When this happened the man who I was writing a letter for would sometimes leap up and thump my assailant hard on the arm, but sometimes he would just laugh and wink at them. They never got a letter from me again.

One evening, as I peered closer to the page to write in

the dim lamplight of the mess deck, a pasty-faced boy leaned over and spat down the back of my neck. His name was Michael Trellis, and he was a powder monkey for one of the starboard gun crews. Enraged, I leaped up and thumped him hard. In an instant, a bosun's mate stepped over and hit me on the back with his rope.

'If I catch you fighting again, Witchall, you're looking at a flogging.' Then he cuffed the other boy around the head. 'You watch your step too, Trellis, y' snotty urchin.'

The boy gave me an evil smirk. 'I'd have pulverised you if he'd not been around. Better not let me catch you alone in the hold.'

Silas had been sitting along from me, and saw it all. As Trellis walked past he tripped him up, and the boy fell hard on his face. Silas lifted him roughly to his feet.

'Sorry, lad, what an unfortunate accident,' he said with unmistakable menace. 'You are in the wars today.' It was enough to let Trellis know I had friends who would look after me, but I wondered if there was more of this to come.

A week into the voyage, as we sat around the mess table at dinnertime, Edmund Ackersley was telling us of strange noises he once heard coming from the depths of the ocean.

'Frightful sounds they was, like a whole army o' lost

souls, wailin' in torment. We reckoned them were a warnin' to mend our sinful ways. And, by 'eck, it were! Within a week we 'ad two men fall from the riggin', and another killed by a loose gun.'

Just then, a boy sitting further down the table from us began to laugh. I did not know him, but he was a friend of Tom Nisbit. 'Did these warnings sound like this, by any chance?' said the boy in an accent I did not recognise. And he bellowed a deep, keening moan.

'You heard them too!' said Ackersley.

'Them's not lost souls,' said the boy, in cocky imitation of Ackersley's Lancashire grammar. 'Them's whales. I've seen them breaching off Newfoundland. They make that noise when they're looking for a mate.'

Ackersley didn't take to being corrected. Quick as a flash, he brought the knife he was using to cut his meat down on the boy's sleeve, pinning his arm to the table. Then he put his face right next to his. 'Them's lost souls, Sonny Jim. Whales be buggered.'

The boy was quite cool-headed about it. 'Whatever you say, chum. Lost souls it is.'

After we'd eaten I walked up to the forecastle with him. I discovered he was an American who was also in the afterguard larboard watch.

'Good day to you, Sam Witchall,' he said with a smile, and shook my hand. 'My name is Richard Buckley.'

I was surprised to find an American boy on a British man-o'-war.

'So, what's an American doing on the *Miranda*?' I asked.

'Oh, I'm not the only one,' he said. 'There's three or four of us. Haven't you met Binns and Woodruff? They're on the forecastle in the starboard watch.'

I hadn't.

'Me, I'm learning my trade,' he said. 'Been aboard the *Miranda* for a year now. I'd like to go back to Boston one day, and an officer post in a merchantman. May even try for a commission in the United States Navy. And what of you, Sam?' he asked me. 'What made you take to the sea?'

'I want to do something with my life,' I told him. 'There's not much to look forward to in the village I come from. My father wanted me to be a schoolteacher and help out in my uncle's shop.'

'That can't be bad, surely?' said Richard. 'Not so that you'd rather be here than there?'

'No, but there's got to be more to life than Wroxham. Don't suppose you've heard of it?' He hadn't. 'We had one moment of excitement every month, when me and my father and brother took our horse and cart to Norwich – it's the big city in those parts.' As I spoke, it already felt like a lifetime ago. 'We went to buy the fancier provisions for my father's shop – tea, coffee and spices mainly. Clip-clop for hours on end, down the rickety road to Norwich. My mother never came with us. She hasn't left the parish in her whole life.'

'So what's so great about Norwich?' asked Richard.

'I love Norwich,' I gushed. 'It's so different. It bustles and buzzes and there are shops selling everything you could ever want. It stinks, though – rotten vegetables, dung, coal fires – but you can't have everything just right, can you?'

'Sounds just like Boston, 'cept that's a seaboard port,' said Richard, and looked a little misty-eyed. 'I used to beg my mom to take me down to the harbour, just so I could gaze at all the tall ships packed together along the quayside, and wonder what it would be like to sail off over the horizon . . .'

I thought wistfully of Norwich. Whenever I went there I realised I could not be a country boy for ever.

'Hey, you're not listening!' Richard laughed.

'I'm a bit like you,' I said. 'My mother always said I was too inquisitive for my own good.'

'She's right,' he said. 'There's too much to see in the world!' Then he looked out to sea and grew reflective. 'I took quite a gamble coming on this ship. Your navy's supposed to be the best in the world, and my grandpa persuaded my dad that a few years' service on a British man-o'-war would set me up for the rest of my life. He might be right, but the trick is to stay alive. Mandeville's an ambitious son of a bitch – who knows what trouble he'll lead us into. Meanwhile, I just behave like a model seaman, especially with the ship's officers. It's all a game, isn't it? I'm damned if I'm letting those stuck-ups get to flog me. So I smile politely, do as I'm asked, and keep my nose clean.'

Despite his bad start with Edmund Ackersley, Richard often joined Ben and our crew to sit and chat on a Sunday afternoon. I was fascinated by Richard's accent, and the words he used. He said 'clever' when he meant 'good', 'mad' when he meant 'angry' and 'closet' when he meant 'cupboard'. But we understood each other well enough. He called the marines 'lobsterbacks', and employed words in a way that made me smile. 'Is there anyone else aboard the ship,' he'd say, 'who comes from your neck of the woods?'

Two weeks into the voyage the pain of my broken tooth became a constant distraction. I could put off a visit to Dr Claybourne no longer. I was reluctant to see him as I was deeply suspicious of medical men. When I was eight I had a sickness which left me weak and dizzy. A doctor friend of the Reverend Chatham came to see me and took me for a walk to the village pond. When I was least expecting it, he pushed me into the water. I dragged myself out, covered in mud and vegetation, and ran home. He followed me back, told my mother to make me drink a small bottle of gin, and then to rest. I forced the gin down, and my head spun so much when I laid it on my pillow that I was violently sick. The shock, explained the doctor, would do me good. After that I had a high fever for a day, but was up and about by the end of the week. I'm sure I got better despite his attentions.

Claybourne was actually more pleasant than our first meeting had suggested. He was gruff, but not without an amiable air. His Scottish accent was so broad I had difficulty understanding him.

He held his surgery every morning on the orlop deck, which was beneath the waterline at the bow of the ship. That day there were just three of us waiting to see him, and I noticed he was sitting with a weary-looking young man who was obviously learning his trade. Claybourne talked to him throughout, barely paying attention to the patients before him. In front of me was one of the maintopmen, whom I gathered was suffering from a hernia.

Claybourne had him lower his trousers, and began gingerly to feel around his groin. 'Yes, there's quite a wee lump there, my man.'

Then he turned to his apprentice. 'Ye offen get the topmen coming wi' hernias from their liftin' the sails,' he explained. 'At port it's broken heeds and the pox. At sea, hernias and scurvy. Later on, ye'll ge' a fair few of them comin' down here with loose teeth and sores from the scurvy. I give 'em more lemon juice t' top up their ration, and tha' usually does the trick. But if ye gave 'em more of the juice before they got the scurvy, then – well, they wouldnae ge' it! But the Captain won't be swayed. It's too great an expense, he says, t' ge' in more lemons than we're already issued with. Only a few of the crew seem to ge' it, he says. So why treat the lot of them? I says, "it's an easier thing to keep a crew healthy, than it is for me to cure 'em", but it falls on deaf ears.'

He produced a sturdy wool and canvas undergarment from among his bags and boxes and spoke to the top-man. 'Ye'll wear this, my man. It's called a truss, and it'll help support your little problem. I can recommend the smoking of tobacco to take off the tension and provide a laxative. An' if that doesnae work, ye'll have to come back an' have ye intestines filled with tepid water. That seldom fails tae produce a beneficial effect.'

The fellow scurried away with a tug of the forelock. I wondered if Claybourne had told him the last bit to discourage him from coming again.

Next up was a forecastleman complaining of vomiting and diarrhoea. He was sent on his way with a dose of blue vitriol which Claybourne quickly fished out of his medicine chest. No sooner had the patient hurried up the ladder than Claybourne turned to his assistant and said, 'That'll kill or cure him soon enough.'

Then it was me. 'Sit yerself down, laddie.' I opened

my mouth, and Claybourne poked around with a grubby finger and a thin needle implement that gleamed silver in the lantern light. 'Well, that's nae guntae ge' any better,' he said with great authority. Then he turned to his assistant. 'Mr McDowell, what shall we do next?'

The young man had obviously been studying hard. 'Standard extraction, sir, with Clef Anglais. Then perhaps the goat's foot elevator, if the tooth cracks and leaves the root in the gum.'

Although I knew the tooth was going to have to come out, I winced at their thoughtless ruminations.

'Aye,' said Claybourne. 'Let's get to work. You can be mother.'

With that the doctor handed me a bottle of brandy. 'Take a good slug, laddie. As much as ye can keep down.' I guzzled the fiery liquid and it sat burning in my stomach. I was not used to strong liquor, and felt I was going to be sick. But that passed, and was followed by a pleasant floating sensation. Then, all at once, Claybourne was standing behind me, holding my head steady in a tight lock with his left arm. 'Open wide,' he crooned, and clamped my lower jaw open with his right hand.

McDowell quickly placed a wooden-handled implement in my mouth and started to rock it to and fro. With every motion I felt an agonising wrench in my jaw, and began to make little yelping noises. Then there was an excruciating jolt – almost like a flash of lightning – so sharp I could almost taste it, as the tooth broke away.

'Steady now,' said Claybourne. 'Here, have another mouthful o' this.' I gulped down more of the brandy. McDowell began to poke around with a pincer-like instrument.

Both men assumed their previous positions. The pain was so intense I wondered if being flogged could be any worse. Amid my agonised cries, McDowell pulled something out, and my mouth filled with blood. 'Spit in this,' said Claybourne matter of factly, holding a small enamelled iron bowl. McDowell held up his fearsome implement before me. Between its jaws was a small sliver of tooth root with a glob of flesh still attached to it.

'Got the rascal,' he said with no small delight. 'Just two more to go.' The next minute was probably the most painful in my life, as he gouged away at my bruised and bleeding gum. But out the roots came, and I was put to sit in the corner of the deck with the bowl.

'Spit away, lad,' said Claybourne. 'When that stops bleeding y' can spend a few hours in sick bay.'

McDowell helped me walk back to the ship's sick bay, a small berth walled in with panels of strong canvas. He had another ship's boy fetch my hammock, and there I stayed for the rest of the morning in the company of two other seamen. One slept and the other spent his time coughing or spitting into a white enamel mug. Ben and

Richard both paid me a brief visit, but I felt too ill to talk to them. My jaw ached terribly, my head pounded from the brandy, and I had no appetite for dinner. Then in the early afternoon, I heard a shout I had been dreading since the voyage began.

'Sail ho!'

CHAPTER 5

Treacherous Waters

I lay in my hammock listening intently, wondering what would happen next. Shortly after, Ben came again to see me.

'You've picked a fine time to be poorly,' he teased. 'We've spotted a French ship. Mandeville's chasing after her. We might catch up with her by late afternoon.'

I buried my head in my hands. Of all the bad moments . . . and us only two weeks out at sea. I felt consumed by my own misery. 'Ben, I can hardly stand up without feeling sick, and my jaw is throbbing . . .'

'Y' wont notice so much when y' get hit by a cannonball,' he said with a wink. 'C'mon. Out on the deck. Some fresh air'll bring the colour back t' your cheeks.' So I staggered up on deck and wandered around the forecastle in the damp, cold afternoon, holding on to Ben's arm to stop myself falling over.

Ben pointed to the enemy ship – a distant silhouette heading away from us towards the coast of Brittany. 'Looks like a corvette. Quite a bit smaller than us. Maybe twenty guns, maybe less. She's been out looking for British merchant ships, I shouldn't wonder. Didn't bank on having us chase her, did she? There's a couple of small fishing ports round this part of the coast, so she's probably heading for one of them.'

I tried to take all this in, but the effort and the swell of the ship just made me feel sick. It was lucky we were so near the heads. I ran over, and retched up a stream of bloody vomit through the netting and into the wake of the ship. Ben swiftly followed on, and held one of my arms to stop me toppling in.

'You've swallowed a lot of blood, Sam. Never mind. Now that's gone, you'll feel a lot better.'

Sadly not. After that I could barely stand, and began to shiver uncontrollably. Lieutenant Spencer had observed the whole scene. 'Best take him back to sick bay, Lovett,' he said to Ben. 'We can leave him there until we're called to quarters.'

I returned to my hammock and listened out for the

commands of the officers, as the *Miranda* tried to gain on her prey. If we made the most of the south-easterly wind, it was possible we would catch the corvette before she reached the safety of the shore.

I wondered if I ought to feel more afraid. After all, this ship was trying to outrun us, rather than eager to fight us. But then I thought of our own battle with the *Isabelle*. We'd only had a single gun, yet we'd inflicted considerable damage on our enemy. When we attacked, would it be me who was floored by grapeshot, or felled by a sniper in the rigging? Our victory was almost guaranteed, but that didn't mean some of us would not be killed.

Although these anxious thoughts circled round my head I still felt weak and drowsy. Soon I drifted off into a half sleep, and woke feeling a little stronger. When one of Dr Claybourne's assistants came to give me bread and water, I found my appetite had returned. Claybourne came round to inspect his patients shortly before supper.

'Off y' go, laddie,' was all he said to me.

Down on the mess deck I was surprised to find the whole crew in a state of excitement. They seemed to be looking forward to the coming battle.

'There'll be prize money in this,' said Edmund Ackersley.

'If we catch them,' said Ben.

This was something I knew only a little about. Ben filled me in. 'Prize money's what the Navy pays for a captured ship. It can add up to thousands of pounds. The captain gets a quarter or more. Then the rest of the ship's officers get a quarter between them. Then the midshipmen and some of the petty officers get an eighth. What's left, that's the last quarter, is split between the rest of the crew. It's not much when it's divided between hundreds of us able and ordinary seamen, but it's certainly better than nothing.'

Richard, canny as he was, knew exactly why the prize money was divided as it was. 'It's the people on the ship who make the decision to attack that get the most money. They've got the most to gain by facing up to a fight rather than avoiding one.'

James Kettleby was more upbeat about the prize money. 'Sometimes a crew gets lucky,' he said. 'We do get much less than the officers, but it can still add up to a year's pay! Me brother told us one lot got a hundred pounds each when their ship captured a French brig full o' treasure. That'd keep a man drunk for an entire six months, and still leave him enough change for a good funeral.'

Tom was more cynical. 'Hundred pounds? Never! That's about six years' pay. But whatever it is, the prize money should be split better than that. We all stand an equal chance of getting killed or maimed. And most captains are wealthy men, anyway – they hardly need the money . . .'

'Don't go counting your chickens,' said Ben. 'It'll be dark in an hour, and I don't think we're going to catch this corvette before nightfall. By the morning she'll have scurried off into port.'

Ben was right. By nightfall we were approaching the coast and the *Miranda* was still too far away from the French ship for us to be called to quarters. But Mandeville was not done yet. When the light was too poor to see our quarry, he had the ship drop anchor, and wait until dawn.

We spent a restless night, with the threat of combat still hanging over the crew. Despite their bravado, I noticed that far more of the men than usual were visited by nightmares, and our brief rest was frequently punctuated by the cries of tormented sleepers. I could barely sleep, anyway. My jaw was throbbing horribly, and I was too anxious.

The following day we took the morning watch from four till eight. When the first light of dawn crept over the horizon we peered through drifting pockets of mist and were surprised to see that the French corvette was no more than a mile ahead of us. Her sails were furled, she was listing slightly to starboard and going nowhere.

Ben peered through the gathering light. 'She's grounded, Sam, or maybe caught on the rocks. I wonder what Mandeville's got up his sleeve now?'

Throughout those groggy early hours, we edged nearer and nearer the corvette. A sailor was placed on the *Miranda*'s bow, to take soundings with a lead weight. He called out the fathoms with a dull regularity, his voice piercing the silence of the grey autumn morning. Although we too were in danger of running aground, Mandeville and his lieutenants seemed coolly confident as they piloted their frigate forward.

Ben looked worried. 'These are treacherous waters, with shallows and rocks to navigate. We get too close in and we're really done for.'

Over on the quarterdeck Mandeville peered though his telescope. Then he called over two of his lieutenants. They both looked too. Ben guessed what was coming.

'I'll bet that ship's been abandoned. Mandeville'll keep us just out of range of her guns, and send a boat over to check.'

A minute later, Middlewych came over to us. 'Mr Lovett. I want your gun crew to join myself and four marines. We're going to take one of the cutters and see what's happening.'

The boat, kept in the waist of the *Miranda*, was swiftly lowered into the water. We clambered aboard – Ben, Tom, James, Oliver, Edmund and me. All six of us shivering in the breeze that blew over the water. It was so cold I almost forgot about my aching jaw.

We each took an oar. Fortunately the sea was still, with almost no swell. 'You'll warm up soon enough, Samuel,' said Oliver Macintosh, 'once we start this rowing.' Then four marines joined us, sitting stiffly in the stern, each carrying a musket. Middlewych squeezed himself into the bow, telescope in hand.

'Slowly does it, men,' he cautioned us. 'We could easily be heading into a trap.'

As we rowed away, I heard the *Miranda*'s drummer boy call the crew to quarters. Mandeville was taking no chances, and had decided to rouse the men who were still sleeping. There was now a frenzy of activity aboard the ship. Within five minutes, the gun ports had been opened, and the *Miranda* began slowly to close the distance between herself and the corvette.

It was an eerie feeling, pulling away from the *Miranda* through the mist, especially as we were looking down the barrels of all her starboard guns. We rowed with our backs to the corvette, so we relied on Middlewych to let us know what was happening. Standing in the bow and peering through his telescope, he kept up a reassuring commentary to no one in particular, partly perhaps to keep his own fear at bay.

'Nothing going on on deck,' he said. 'She looks completely deserted. Gun ports open, but can't see anyone manning the guns . . . Now the mist's closed around her . . .'

As we grew nearer, my trepidation increased. I desperately wanted to look round and see the ship we were approaching, but if I did this I would break my stroke and incur the wrath of Middlewych and my fellow oarsmen. The tension was unbearable. For now, all I could hear was the splash of oar in water, the laboured exertions of my fellow rowers and the faint crash of waves on a distant beach. At any moment I expected the crack of a musket. I was convinced the French were lying in wait for us aboard their ship and even now a marksman was training his musket on the back of my head.

The mist cleared again and Middlewych began his leisurely commentary. 'Still can't see a soul . . .'

The blast of a couple of guns cut short his next words. I nearly jumped out of my skin. James let go of his oar and cursed both our luck and his clumsiness. Tom lost his too. Middlewych ducked instinctively as cannon shots whistled low over our heads, so close we felt the turbulence in the air.

Seconds later, two plumes of water shot up in the sea, halfway between us and the *Miranda*. The corvette had fired too soon.

'Lie as flat as you can,' shouted Middlewych urgently. We all knew what was coming. As we tried desperately to squeeze into the bottom of our cutter, all ten of the

Miranda's starboard 18lb guns roared out in a single broadside. It was an awesome sound and it produced an awesome result. As soon as our shots had whistled over our heads to crash and splinter into their target we peered over the gunwale to survey the damage. Judging by the still settling plumes of water, only three shots had fallen short. The rest had mauled the upper deck, leaving ugly holes all along the length of the ship.

'Keep down, keep down,' shouted Middlewych impatiently. 'We're quite near enough for musket shots.' Then he peered cautiously over the bow. 'We'll just have to wait here, and see what happens.' He sounded not a little rattled. Then he picked up his telescope and trained it again on the corvette.

Much to my surprise, I heard him laugh. 'They're scuttling off! They're going over the larboard side. Probably still got a boat there!'

Relief swept over me. If this was true, we might all live to see the end of the day. 'Keep down, though. There'll be another broadside from the *Miranda* any second now.'

But that broadside never came. Mandeville must have been able to see the French gunners abandoning their ship too. He didn't want to inflict too much damage on his prize, and the *Miranda* held her fire.

We waited another few minutes, then Middlewych stood up with his telescope to get a better view. 'There they go, heading for the shore.' We had drifted nearer to the bow of the corvette, and I could see a packed launch pulling away. 'Right, then, let's go in and have a good look at her.'

In the panic that followed the first shots, we had lost two oars in the water. I was proud to say I'd kept a hold on mine, but James, who'd lost his, took over my oar anyway.

'Brawn over brains,' he said with a wink.

Free from the oars, I now had the chance to have a good look at the ship. She was a beauty. Like us she had three masts, but she was much shorter in length. Sleek and low in the water, her hull was painted a fetching green, with a band of gold above and below the gun ports.

'She'll make a handsome prize,' said Edmund.

'That depends on whether we can get her moving,' Middlewych sighed.

But as I gazed at this beautiful ship the bright flash of an explosion burst deep inside her, sending black splinters high into the air. The noise rolled like dirty thunder across the waves. At first I wondered if the *Miranda* had fired again, but Middlewych called on us all to lie flat again.

Almost at once another much louder explosion rent the air, and we all felt the heat of the blast on our backs. Something crashed into the sea right next to us, large enough to rock our boat and drench us with freezing water. When debris stopped falling, I dared to take a look. Part of a yardarm, sail still furled around it, bobbed nearby. A large plume of black smoke was billowing up from the wreckage of the corvette, and flames were beginning to gnaw at what was left of her upper deck.

'Damn it,' said Middlewych. 'Rascals have blown up their ship.'

Ben spoke glumly. 'I'll bet they put a fuse on gunpowder barrels in the magazine. There goes our prize money.'

'Cheer up, Ben,' I couldn't help saying. 'At least we weren't on the ship when it blew up.'

With the merest shrug Middlewych turned us round, to head back to the *Miranda*. It had been quite a morning, and it was not yet eight o'clock.

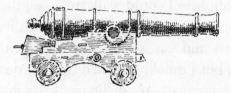

CHAPTER 6

B is for Boarder

A month into the voyage, I was coming up the companionway from the gun deck to the upper deck when a novel thought entered my head. I liked it up here. To go from the enclosed, stifling world of the mess deck and out into the salty sea air and sunshine was one of life's pleasures. It also dawned on me that I was no longer in a state of constant anxiety. True, at any moment the *Miranda* could be called to quarters, and I could never be certain when I woke that I would live to see the evening, but I had at least begun to master the duties required of me and adjust to the ship's exhausting routine.

When off duty I could walk freely on the forward part of the upper deck, along the waist with its ship's boats, spare masts and yards lain over the opening above the gun deck, but I quickly learned that the quarterdeck was forbidden territory to ordinary seamen who had no business being there.

Whenever I made my way to the upper deck I would marvel at the agility of the topmen – those of us in the ship's crew who worked up in the sails. They seemed to revel in the danger of their work – running along the narrow lengths of the yardarms, and dropping down to the thin foot rope beneath the yard, which was all that lay between them and the dizzying drop to the deck. They would swing from one mast to another on the stays, and slide down to the deck on the halyards. They seemed as confident in the rigging as a squirrel running through the branches of a horse chestnut. Topmen had something of the flair of circus acrobats – we called their antics 'skylarking'. I once heard Lieutenant Middlewych remark with some pride to a midshipman that he was sure people would pay money to watch our topmen perform.

Occasionally, I would be called upon to set or furl a sail. It was here that I first met a mizzentopman called Joseph Neil. Almost exactly my age, Joseph was from Yorkshire and walked with a cocky swagger. I'd grown increasingly unsure of myself up among the rigging. Joseph noticed this when I first went up with him, and chided me.

'Come on, y' big jellyfish,' he sneered, then winked to take the sting from his taunt. Seeing I was shaky, he drew level with me and said, 'One hand for the Navy. One hand for yourself. That's how to make sure y' don't fall off.'

Like me he had joined a merchant ship. He sailed out of Scarborough but had been pressed into the Navy. As I got to know him better, I helped him write home. Sometimes when we talked he would drop his cocksure front, and I started to like him.

'Course it's terrifying up there,' he admitted to me once. 'Especially in a storm, with a gale pushing and pulling you to and fro, and all you've got between you and your maker is a wet slippery rope to hold on to. Last year I had to go up to the main topgallant through a freezing fog. Ice on the rigging! My hands just went numb. You always know when you go up that you'll come down – but you never know whether it'll be the hard or the easy way.'

Joseph picked up his swagger from the other men in his watch. They were an evil lot, who could shame the devil with their curses. I'd occasionally sit with Joseph and them on a Sunday afternoon, and they would often talk about what they would do when we ran into a

French or Spanish ship. They seemed to revel in the violence they would inflict on Johnny Foreigner, and their humour often left me wondering when I was supposed to laugh.

They were equally merciless with their own kind, and spoke with scorn of any comrade who had fallen from the rigging. 'Remember that pipsqueak the press gang picked up last year?' said one of the lads. 'Him from Dorset that fell off the fore topgallant.' Another of them adopted an expression of sheer terror, and flailed his arms like a windmill in a gale, and they all began to laugh.

These were men who would joke about their own execution, and believe me, it was a racing certainty that some of them would end their life dangling from a yardarm. They seemed to have a pact between them that even on the gallows they would try to outdo each other in devil-may-care japery. 'When Stephen and George were hanged together,' said another of the topmen, 'after that carry on with Lieutenant Fisher, they had a little bet about who would be the last to piss himself when they were swinging from the yardarm.' At this point Joseph filled me in – explaining that men who are hung lose control of their bladders, usually at the point of death.

At first I thought them a crude and cruel bunch, but I knew enough to keep my feelings hidden. Living so close to death they turned their plight into an endless amusement – where even their own execution could be turned into some laddish stunt to outdo each other. Even their curses began to amuse me. One evening, I was up with one of Joseph's watch in the mizzen topsail. 'Stay tied, you buggering lopsided dog!' he said, in disgust at a disintegrating rope he was using to furl the sail.

Although I was intrigued by these rough and ready men, I felt more comfortable with my own gun crew. They seemed a more easy-going bunch. As I got to know them, I discovered that all my messmates had a special keepsake or charm they hoped would bring them luck. They kept them hidden in their wooden trunks and canvas ditty-bags. There, alongside the sewing needles, spools of thread, buttons, letters and spare clothes, lay these small tokens of life away from our uncertain world. Sometimes after supper, one of them would bring out their keepsake and tell us the story that went with it.

Tom had a horn beaker with the face of an eagle carefully carved into the side. 'Brought that back from New York. Red Indian, it is, though I don't know which tribe.'

James had a small ivory locket with the words 'Not lost but gone before' inlaid around the edge. It had a hinged lid with a compartment containing a short strand of braided hair tied at each end with a sliver of red cotton. One evening, when he had drunk a little more than was wise, he got out the braid and laid it over the palm of his hand. 'There's three strands there. Me, me missus and our Kate.' I looked hard and there they were. One fair like James, one dark and the other brown. 'That's all that's left of her, that strand of brown hair. Carried away by scarlatina, she was. Eight years old . . . We both watched her breathe her last . . .' That was all he said. We all felt the weight of his sadness.

After a while, Ben sought to change the mood by showing us what he kept with him. It was a small double-heart brooch, inlaid with garnets.

'My missus gave us that on our wedding day. It was her grandma's. She says it'll keep me safe, and it's worked so far.'

'All these keepsakes – some of them are quite valuable, aren't they?' I said to Ben.

'No, I don't think so,' he said. 'Most of them aren't worth much, to be honest. But there's a lot of faith invested in them. And for the man who has one . . . well, you couldn't put a price on it.'

Richard and me were quietly amused by how superstitious these hardened seamen were. We were certainly careful to say nothing when the men talked about the *Flying Dutchman* – at least three had claimed to have seen it – or mermaids.

'Right up to the ship they came,' said Ben lasciviously.

'I saw 'em bobbing up and down, in the wake of the stern. Real beauty, one of 'em. And not a stitch on her, save for a seaweed necklace.'

After these discussions Richard would take me to one side and mimic the older men's wide-eyed superstition or lechery. 'We've got to get out while we're young, Sam,' he'd say. I liked his cynicism for all things supernatural, although here he was almost alone among us ordinary seamen. Practically every man aboard could claim he had seen a ghost on the ship. When night fell aboard the *Miranda*, most of us feared the flickering shadows, and staircases that vanished into the dark pool of the hold. The ship was a man-o'-war, and a lot of terrible things had happened aboard her. Men had fallen from the rigging, been crushed by their cannon, flogged to death, and torn apart in battle. I sometimes wondered if there was any one spot on the ship that, at one time or another, had not been the scene of some hellish torment.

Although life at sea was made up of myriad everyday trials and dangers, I learned to appreciate its pleasures too, especially when we took our rest before bed or on a Sunday afternoon. Sometimes a man would sing or play a fiddle or whistle – a gentle lament or lullaby for the dimming day. Colm played a lovely melody called 'Wexford Bay'. The tune moved me. Music at this time of day was always quiet. But on Sunday afternoons, which we had to ourselves if we were not taking the afternoon watch, it would be more raucous. Then, some of the men would dance and sing.

One of the most enthusiastic dancers was a fellow I had noticed on my first night on the *Miranda*, who had the crucifixion depicted on his back, among other tattoos. Most of these were Biblical quotations of an unforgiving nature – 'Burning for burning, wound for wound, stripe for stripe' and 'With the jaw of an ass have I slain a thousand men'. I discovered his name was Vincent Thomas and I always thought of him as 'Vengeful Tattoos'. As I tried to decipher some of the smaller quotations as he spun around, he caught my eye and dragged me up to dance. 'My, but you've got a pretty mouth,' he whispered as he whirled me around. I took care not to look at him too closely after that.

As September turned to October we were blessed with a final spell of mild weather. Richard and I made the most of it by sitting up on the forecastle during our rest time between watches, although we were always careful what we said when officers and bosun's mates were within earshot.

Sometimes Richard told me about his country. It was, he said, a land of broad rivers and endless meadows and woodland. He told me about the Red Indians of America, and the troubled relationship they had with the European settlers. The names of their tribes –

Cherokee, Arapaho, Conestoga – spoke of an alien yet fascinating world.

'So how long have your family been in America?' said Tom Shepherd, who sometimes joined us.

'Forty, fifty years. My ma and pa both came to Boston when they were babes in arms. My ma was born in Bristol, my pa in Liverpool. Grandpa Buckley still considers himself a loyal British citizen. He loved it when I enlisted for this game. "Get some Frenchmen for me boy!" That was the last thing he said when I left.' Then Richard lowered his voice to a whisper and leaned close to me. 'Can't say I've got anything against the French, myself – especially as they helped us win our independence – no offence meant to you fellows. Grandpa still feels quite distressed about the revolution, and gets maudlin when he's had a few slugs of whisky. But he's done well for himself in Boston, and he's too set in his ways to think about going back to England.'

Although Richard was careful not to show it openly, he had a particular dislike for the *Miranda*'s officers, especially the Captain and his lieutenants, and the way they regarded themselves as superior beings. 'You hear them talking,' he said to me when we were alone, 'and the worse thing is, most of you English go along with it. You believe they are better than you!'

Sitting in the sun on the forecastle on one such an afternoon, we started chatting to Joseph Neil, a mizzenmast topman. Joseph liked to boast, and he was keen to talk about a girlfriend he had back home. He produced a lock of blonde plaited hair, tied in a blue ribbon, which he carried in the top pocket of his shirt. 'Ower lass', he called her. She was from Scarborough, he said, and the two had known each other since they could walk.

Richard seemed surprised that a boy so young should have a girlfriend. 'Can't say I've much time for girls,' he said nonchalantly.

Joseph took his indifference as a cue for sympathy. 'Never you mind, Richard,' he said. 'There's plenty of fish int' sea.'

'Who wants to court a fish?' said Richard.

'And 'ow about you, Sam. D'you have a girl at 'ome?'

I wasn't going to be outdone. 'She's called Rosie. Last I saw of her was in the spring, but as soon as we get off this ship, I'm going straight up to Yarmouth to see her again.'

'She'll be an old maid by the time you get off this ship, Sam,' teased Richard, 'or married with five snotty-nosed brats.' They both began to badger me for more details. Then Peter Lyons, one of the starboard forecastle men, came to sit with us. He had a face like thunder.

'We've got a thief on board, lads,' he said to no one in particular. 'Someone's stealing. A painted egg cup here, an ivory box there. One of the fellas has even had a brass button stolen. It's barely worth a penny, but it came from an old shipmate who saved his life . . . There'll be hell to pay if we ever find the bastard who did this.'

'How d'you know it's just one man? What if it's several people?' said Richard.

Lyons was sure of himself. 'I've been on three men-o'-war in my time, and no one steals from their fellow seamen. It's not right and it's not wise . . . It's got to be one man. We'll find him in the end, and then he'll wish he'd never been born.'

It was a sour end to what had been a pleasant conversation. When we returned to our duties I wondered briefly who would be stupid enough to steal from his fellows.

News of the thief spread rapidly. In the mess that night the crew talked of little else. It was trinkets that were being stolen – mainly keepsakes from wives or sweethearts. From what we could make out, three of the victims at least were from the starboard watch, stationed in the forecastle. Among Ben's gun crew those who had anything small of value took to carrying it around in a pocket or on a string around their neck.

That night, as I settled down in my hammock, I thought about the lie I had told my shipmates. Rosie was my friend, it was true, but she wasn't what you'd call a girlfriend. I had last seen her in Great Yarmouth, the night before I joined the *Franklyn*. My father had taken me to stay with his old friend Benjamin Hooke, who lived on the edge of the town, close by the sea. Our family had known Benjamin's family for years, and I had always liked his daughter Rosie. She and I were almost the same age and played happily together – one moment crimson pirates, the next mermaid and merman frolicking in the surf on the nearby beach.

I had not seen Rosie and the Hookes for a couple of years. That evening we had sat down to a splendid feast. Benjamin's wife Anne cooked us a goose, and we children were even allowed a little wine. Throughout the meal Rosie caught my attention as she had never done before.

After we'd eaten, Benjamin had suggested a stroll by the shore to walk off our meal. The beach was just a short walk from the house, and the night was mild. A strong wind blew in from the sea, but it was warm and pleasant. High cloud covered the sky, and moonlight shone through in mottled patches.

Anne, Benjamin and my father had walked ahead, leaving Rosie and I to keep an eye on her two younger sisters, but after a while they ran to their parents, demanding to be carried. Rosie was keen to know what I was going to do, quick to laugh at my stories. After a while we stopped, and walked to the very edge of the sea. The warm wind came in strong along the shore, blowing her dress tight against her slender body. She stared up at the moon as it darted quickly between the scudding clouds. Now we had stopped talking and there was a comfortable silence between us, and I wondered if I dare kiss her. I had never kissed a girl before. In fact, until that evening, I had never even thought of kissing a girl before. Then my father had shouted over to us from a hundred yards ahead, 'Come along, Sam,' and the moment passed. But the next morning, as I had prepared to leave, Rosie asked me to write to her when I could, and let her know how I was finding my life at sea.

I had left the house feeling like I was walking on air. I wrote to her a couple of times from the *Franklyn*, but no post ever came back. On the *Franklyn* George assured me that letters often took months to catch up with a coastal merchantman. Now I supposed it would be even more difficult for post to catch a patrolling frigate.

I slowly lost my fear of the heavy guns. If I kept my wits about me I knew I should be able to keep myself from injury. But the prospect of hand-to-hand fighting still haunted me. I had no idea how to defend myself if anyone attacked me, so I was pleased when Ben told me I was to be trained in the use of hand-held weapons.

This took place in the afternoons after dinner, and I was usually accompanied by Richard. Our instructor was Sergeant Oates of the marines. He would line up the sailors like soldiers, and talk about these fearful instruments and their gruesome purpose in a clipped, matter-of-fact tone – almost as if we were being instructed in the finer points of carpentry.

Of the pike he'd say, 'Thrust and withdraw. Short sharp prod. That's all you need.' Of the pistol, 'Discharge at no less than ten yards for full effect. Once discharged it can be used as a club.' Then he'd produce a cutlass. 'Slash and jab, but mind your guard. Never raise your arm above the shoulder.'

The tomahawk seemed to fascinate him, maybe because it was a recent addition to the Royal Navy arsenal. 'A useful weapon in a melee, especially when directed against the side of the head. If you have two such instruments, the spike opposite the blade is useful for hauling yourself up the side of an enemy ship.'

I marvelled at the idea that a sailor could row over to another vessel, then haul himself up the side just using two tomahawks to make a series of holds. Then, if he managed to get to the deck, have the strength to fight for his life.

When we had been instructed in the use of the weapons, we would be taught fencing steps to ensure our effectiveness with the cutlass. Richard and I called these movements 'ballet lessons'. At first I could not take them seriously, but these steps had a deadly purpose. The more nimble the cutlass wielder, the more likely he was to survive in hand-to-hand combat. Many of the steps were designed to put as much distance as possible between the man with the cutlass and his opponent.

I made good progress, and Richard was a natural. After observing us in our drill, I heard Mandeville remark to Lieutenant Spencer, 'Yes, put a B against both their names.' I wondered what on earth he meant. Spencer returned soon after to explain.

'Congratulations, boys,' he said cheerily. 'You're now both designated boarders.'

My heart sank, and the creeping fear I had felt all through the first month aboard the ship returned. 'B' stood for boarder – men whose duty it was to swarm over to an enemy vessel during combat, when the captain called out, 'Boarders away!' I should have known that showing any skill in this deadly art was a mistake.

Silas confirmed my fears. 'I'm staying well out of that, Sam. Having a B against your name brings you no special privileges or extra pay. But it's more likely you'll be killed when we go into action.'

Ben wasn't having this. 'Don't you worry, lad. I'm a boarder too and I'll look after you in a scrap. Being a boarder will get you noticed by the Captain or lieutenants. If you fight well and bravely, you may find yourself promoted.'

I felt inclined to agree with Silas. I knew I could be

killed if we attacked another ship, but had convinced myself that if I was careful with my cartridge box, this was unlikely. It had never occurred to me that I might be sent over to another ship to fight in hand-to-hand combat.

From that moment onward I felt I was fated to die or suffer some hideous injury. Some nights I would lie in my hammock twitching my toes or wiggling my fingers. 'Be grateful you have all your limbs, Sam,' I'd say to myself. 'One day, you might have to do without some of them.' I'd wonder what it would be like to have a leg or an arm off, or watch the world with only one eye.

The day the *Isabelle* had come to get me still lingered in my dreams. I tried not to think about what it would feel like to be disembowelled with a cutlass, and then swiftly turfed over the side of the ship to drown and bleed to death in freezing water. I prayed that if I had to die, it would be a swift end – cut in two or beheaded by a cannonball, or dashed to death on the deck after a fall from the topgallant.

Despite these dark thoughts, the time I had lying in my hammock was still my favourite part of the ship's day. Alone at last in this tide of humanity, I would close my eyes and wait for sleep to carry me away. Unless it had been a sunny day, this was the only time I felt warm. Cold and damp was as much a part of life aboard the *Miranda* as the daily scrubbing and drilling. As we lay in our hammocks, the master-at-arms and his corporals would creep by, extinguishing any stray light. Beneath the low rumble of a hundred and fifty sleeping men I could hear the sea wash against the side of the ship, the forlorn ring of the ship's bell as it marked each passing half hour, and even the creaking of the rigging. Once a fortnight or so, during this middle evening time, two of the officers in the gunroom would play flute and cello duets. I never found out who it was who played or who wrote these melodies, but the music they made was like nothing I had heard in Wroxham – flowing lines that intertwined one over the other, twisting in long graceful curves, like two courting gulls riding the currents in a summer afternoon sky.

When I listened to this music I would yearn for home or wonder what Rosie was doing. I could imagine her walking along the beach where I had last seen her, the wind blowing her frock tight against her body. Perhaps she would turn her face to the sinking sun, and allow the pale evening light to caress the curve of her cheek. Maybe it would be raining, and her hair would be plastered down her face as she hurried home, her cotton dress soaked through to the soft skin beneath. Or maybe she was sitting by the fire at home, candle close to her chair, writing a letter to me. Sometimes, if the day had gone badly, I would wonder if she was out walking with another lad – someone bolder and better than me, who knew how to woo a girl. Perhaps she'd kiss him, and let him run his hands up and down her dress. I tried not to think of this. I needed to imagine that Rosie was thinking of me just as much as I often thought of her. Then a dreamless sleep would overtake me until the bosun's whistle blew, and another day would come crashing down upon me.

CHAPTER 7

Brutal World

'Just look at that,' said Silas to me one day when we were both on deck, eight weeks out at sea. 'Strutting around like he owns the ship. I bet he's only just stopped sucking his thumb.' He was staring at a young midshipman whose name I did not know. Immaculately dressed in a smart blue coat, similar in style to that of a lieutenant, he was handsome and dark-haired, although his creamy skin was flecked with a few spots and the beginnings of a moustache. I noticed a shiny new dirk dangling from his belt. This was unusual – even among the senior officers. Such was the expense of purchasing a new sword that most officers often carried their father's or even their grandfather's.

Midshipmen were an aspect of the Navy I had known little about. Silas told me they were officers in training – hoping after six years to pass their examination to become a lieutenant. Despite their age and inexperience, they had the same authority as any other ship's officer. Seeing small boys, some with voices not yet broken, cursing and even striking hulking tars, seemed faintly comical. When I first saw this, with Vengeful Tattoos no less, I expected the man to pick up the boy, and hurl him thirty yards out to sea. But he didn't. Any sign of insolence towards a midshipman met with swift retribution. As we discovered.

Silas stared a little too long, and a little too disrespectfully. The midshipman noticed, and stared back with ill-tempered disdain. This was a clear case of dumb insolence. He turned to a bosun's mate, then pointed at Silas and demanded, 'Bosun, start that man,' his voice wavering unsteadily between treble and tenor. In an instant, the bosun stepped forward and delivered a swift lash with his rope.

Silas winced a little, and for a second I thought he was going to utter an oath. I grabbed at his shoulder and hurriedly dragged him away to the bow. 'Say nothing,' I whispered, fearful that a bad-tempered outburst would earn Silas a flogging. He angrily pulled away from me, teeth clenched tight.

When we were out of earshot, Silas seethed quietly to himself. 'The little shit, I'll have him for this.'

That evening I was walking from the forecastle down to the mess deck for supper when I heard a voice right behind me hiss, 'Thief.' It was Michael Trellis, along with a couple of his friends. They all started. 'Thief, Thief, Thief,' in a low hiss. All three of them were Marine Society boys, street urchins sold into the Navy by a parent who could no longer afford to keep them. They stuck together like a tight outlaw family, and unsettled me with their hard stares and brutal manner.

The taunting continued. I walked ahead, trying to shake them off. They followed just behind me, keeping up their whispering. Now my crewmates were beginning to turn and look. 'Thief, Thief, Thief . . .'

I knew I should have ignored them, but I fell into their trap. My temper snapped, and I turned to face them. 'What are you talking about?' I said angrily. 'Why are you calling me a thief?' I tried to sound threatening, but I suspect I sounded more hurt and upset than I intended.

Michael Trellis, sure now he had an audience, spat out his poison. 'Him, he's the thief. I heard tell it's him that's been thievin' them trinkets. Where you got 'em hidden then, Witchall? Somewhere in the hold I'll bet . . .'

I was so surprised by what he said, I could think of no sensible reply. Then Trellis and his boys started to dig their fingers at me. 'Thief, Thief, Thief . . .'

I snapped. 'Get off me, you wretch.' I pushed Trellis in the chest, and he threw himself at me. Before any blows could fall, Silas stormed in to separate the two of us.

Lewis Tuck, the bosun's mate Silas and I had crossed in our first moments aboard the *Miranda*, arrived like a bad penny. He thwacked all three of us with his rope.

'There's no fighting on this ship. What's happening here?' No one said anything. 'Right,' said Tuck. 'Let's take the three of you aft.'

We were swiftly taken to the quarterdeck, where Lieutenant Spencer held sway. He seemed annoyed by this intrusion on his time.

'Now, don't mess me about. I want to know why you two boys were fighting, and why you, Mr Warandel, were involved in this unseemly scuffle.'

Trellis spoke up. I was astounded at his gall. 'Witchall, sir, he's the one who's been stealing things around the ship.'

This was too much. 'That's not true,' I shouted before Tuck cut me short with a smack around the head.

'You'll speak when you're spoken to.'

Spencer looked at Trellis with utter contempt. With some relief I realised he had no regard for the boy's story at all. 'And on what basis do you make this assertion?' he said coldly.

'Somebody told me . . .' said Trellis, 'and I seen him sneaking around.' He was losing his nerve by the second.

Spencer turned to me. 'And what have you got to say, Witchall?'

'This is all a complete lie, sir. I've never stolen anything in my life.' I tried to sound as reasonable as I could.

Spencer turned on the bosun's mate. 'Mr Tuck, why are you bothering me with this schoolboy scrap?'

Tuck began to look flustered. 'I don't think we can count on Witchall's word, sir. I think we ought to search his hammock and his ditty-bag.'

'You couldn't count your balls and get the same answer twice,' said Silas under his breath.

'What was that?' said Tuck, and hit Silas on the back with his rope.

'I said the boy couldn't count on Trellis to answer truthfully, Mr Tuck.'

Tuck looked unconvinced. I had to stifle a huge grin. Silas was really sailing close to the wind with that one.

Spencer had heard enough. 'Mr Tuck. Have these boys clapped in irons for the night. Fighting between seamen will not be tolerated. And you,' he turned to Silas, 'can join them for talking out of turn.'

Tuck and four marines marched us to the gun deck. Close to the main hatchway several shackles had been fitted to the floor, and we were forced to sit on the deck right next to each other while an iron bar was placed around each left leg. When this was done, Tuck gave Silas another belt with his rope and said, 'You can all stay there till the morning watch. And you, Witchall, if I catch you fighting again, you'll be in serious trouble.'

I knew there was no point arguing, and besides, I was uncomfortably close to Michael Trellis. Tuck left, and a single marine brandishing a bayonet stood over us. Trellis started his 'Thief' taunt again, right in my ear, but the marine kicked him hard in the back.

'And that'll go for any one of you who feels like making conversation,' he said.

Spending eleven hours on a draughty wooden deck with one leg locked tightly in irons was a miserable experience, but it was not a flogging. In the dead of night I even managed to snatch some sleep. When we were released at four the next morning, I found I could barely walk for the next few minutes, and my leg ached for days afterwards where it had been held by the iron. But whenever I began to feel sorry for myself I thought of Silas's remark to Tuck and smiled.

At breakfast I told Ben what had happened.

'Trellis and his mates seem to have it in for me, and

Tuck. I've been doing my best to keep out of trouble, and get on with everybody, so I can't understand it.'

'There's no sense in it,' said Ben. 'Maybe Trellis doesn't like you because you've got a mother and father who looked after you? Maybe it's because you can read and write? Lads like him, they've had a rough life, and they're little more than beasts, Sam. I'd keep out of his way if you can help it. As for Tuck – maybe he's got his eye on you because you're a friend of Silas, and he's got him down as a troublemaker.'

The day got worse. When I was out on the upper deck, Lieutenant Spencer beckoned me over.

'You should make more of an effort to keep out of trouble, Witchall,' he said mysteriously. 'Report to the Captain's cabin tomorrow at eleven o'clock.'

I began to shiver, although I did not know whether it was from cold or fear. Did Spencer think I was a thief after all? I felt sick with worry. The morning dragged terribly before I could pour out my fears to Ben over dinner. He was quite calm about it.

'He can't think you're the thief, so you can stop worrying about that.'

Edmund had overheard. 'I wouldn't be so sure. Maybe someone's pointing the finger at you. Maybe the officers just want a culprit and they don't care whether he's guilty or not. If they think it's you, you'll be flogged for sure.'

Ben kicked Edmund under the table. 'Shut it, and stop worrying the lad. I'll tell yer what I think. I think they've found out about your false address.'

That must be it, I told myself. I had written letters to Rosie and my parents during the voyage, and on the previous day the ship's post had been passed over to a homebound British frigate that had crossed our path.

'Don't look too pleased with yerself,' said Edmund. 'Y' can be flogged for lyin' too.'

I spent the rest of the day worrying about what would happen to me, and slept barely a wink that night. Eleven o'clock came round, and I duly reported to the Captain's cabin. Spencer was there, and the Captain, and one of the bosun's mates, who was carrying a rope, broom and shovel. I thought they were going to hang me, and the blood drained from my face.

Mandeville looked at me sternly. 'Why does your parents' address in the muster book not tally with the address on the letters you write to them?'

I stammered an apology, although I tried to keep my dignity. 'I'm sorry, sir. I was confused. It won't happen again.'

'It won't,' said Mandeville plainly. 'There's no more to be said here, Mr Spencer. I'll leave you to deal with the boy.'

I looked at the rope and could imagine it tightening

around my neck. My legs began to tremble and I had to strain every muscle to walk as I was brusquely marched out of the cabin. Spencer told me sternly I was to be hoisted up to the main yard with the rope tied around my waist, and the broom and shovel tied to my back.

'My waist?' I blurted out. 'You mean I'm not going to be hanged?'

Spencer looked at me with some irritation. 'Don't be stupid, Witchall.'

So half an hour before the noon sighting I was hoisted up the mainmast with the rope around my chest. There I was left to dangle for half an hour, whilst anyone passing by was obliged to shout 'Liar, liar' at me. It was cold, and my arms began to ache after ten minutes, but, as I had told myself when I was clapped in irons, at least it wasn't a flogging. In fact, there was more flogging going on beneath me. Most of the ship's crew could not be bothered to shout 'Liar, liar' at me, and a bosun's mate was placed beneath to beat any man with his rope if he did not shout as he passed. When I came down, I was told that this punishment had a second part. I was to clean the heads every day for a fortnight.

'It was probably Spencer that spotted your address,' Ben told me. 'The miserable sod should have let it be. He could have just changed the record, but you must have caught him on a bad day. Probably his piles playing up, I shouldn't wonder.' Ben picked up all sorts of scurrilous information from the officers' servants, which he would occasionally drop into the conversation with us.

Despite having to clean the heads, I was keenly aware I'd got off lightly, not least because Mandeville had a reputation among the crew for being cruel. The previous Sunday evening, two men from the starboard watch had drunk more grog than was good for them, and were arguing loudly about the merits of various loose women in Portsmouth. Mandeville ordered both men to be gagged and tied in the mizzen rigging, faces to the wind. There they spent the next two hours in the teeth of a freezing autumn gale, an iron bit tied tightly across their mouths with a piece of dirty canvas. I thought it an horrendous thing. But Ben pointed out that the Captain could have had both men flogged. They were, after all, clearly drunk.

Silas wasn't having that. 'Listen to God's representative on Earth,' he sneered. 'Is there anything Mandeville would do that you wouldn't excuse him for?'

Ben bristled with anger. He didn't like to have his judgement challenged – especially not in front of the rest of his gun crew. 'What would you know about it, y' lanky streak of piss?' he hissed. 'You're heading for a sticky end, mate. The bosun's mates and the officers have already got you down as a troublemaker, and they're just itching for an excuse to have you flogged.'

This stopped Silas in his tracks. Ben went on, trying to justify himself. 'I don't like Mandeville any more than any other men on our ship. All I'm saying is I've seen far worse.'

We expected random cruelties from the officers. Because they came from a different world than ours we almost accepted it as their natural right. Not so the bosun's mates. They were the most openly despised men on board the *Miranda*, because they were ordinary men like us. We always tensed up when we saw one of them coming. Lewis Tuck was the worst. If he were dimmer I would have said he reminded me of a fairground boxer – the sort who fight allcomers for money, and whose chosen profession has knocked what little sense he had in the first place clean out of his head. But Lewis Tuck was brighter than that, and ambitious. He was young enough to believe he might catch the Captain's eye, and win promotion. But as he could neither read nor write we all knew this was unlikely.

He made it clear he had a special dislike of me. Ben was right. Like Michael Trellis, he seemed to resent the fact that I could read and write. One late afternoon, when I was sitting with a book on the deck, he crept up to me, and gave me a stinging whack with his knotted rope.

'Aren't you a clever boy,' he sneered.

The next morning, when I was making repairs to the deck planking, I accidentally spilled some tar on the deck. As I cursed and began to scrape it off I caught sight of Tuck staring right over at me. His eyes narrowed and he sauntered up to me with a humourless smile upon his lips.

'My dear fellow,' he said, with a mock gentility no doubt inspired by Lieutenant Middlewych, 'permit me to point out that you are spilling tar upon His Majesty's quarterdeck.'

I said nothing in my defence. There was no point enraging him further. I could guess what was coming. Most of the ratings aboard had heard this routine before, and my body started to tense up. I could feel my legs beginning to shake and I fought hard to stop this happening. I was determined not to let him see how afraid I was. He carried on with his speech, looking around with a smirk to see whether or not he was gathering an audience. A few of the crew had indeed stopped to watch. Some were laughing with him.

'This is a deck, I may venture to observe, which has been scrubbed spotless not an hour before.' As he spoke, his voice began to rise in both volume and fury. 'And now, you worthless lubberly dog, I am obliged to do my duty with as much attention as you have failed to do yours.' With that I felt the sharp sting of his rope on my back. Three times he hit me hard. On the third stroke I fell to my knees with the force of the blow. 'Damn you to hell!' he bellowed. 'If I catch you spilling tar again, I'll slice you starboard to larboard with my cutlass!'

When he'd gone, tears flowed down my face. It wasn't the pain of the beating that had upset me, but Tuck's sheer malice. Ben came over and spoke sharply to me.

'Come on, Sam. Y' can't let a brute like that upset you. You'll just encourage him. Dry them tears quick and try to look like you don't care.' Then he started to help scrape up the tar, and his voice softened. 'You don't need other people thinking you're an easy target either, Sam. Plenty o' men on this ship'll make y' life a misery, just to make themselves feel a bit better than you.' I thought of those few others who had stopped to snigger at my plight, and knew he was right.

That night, round the mess table, we talked of Lewis Tuck in hushed voices. Tom Shepherd, as ever, seemed to have the measure of the man.

'He's ambitious, all right, but I'll bet he knows he's going to be a bosun's mate for the rest of his Navy life. There's a bright man and a thug inside Tuck, and the thug always wins.'

Ben butted in. 'He's bound to get his promotion. Mandeville needs men like him to run his ship.'

But Tom was sure of his ground. 'No, the Captain's too smart. Like him or not, Mandeville always punishes a man for a good reason, and with clear intention. Not

Tuck. He takes too much pleasure in handing out his thrashings. If you made him a midshipman or an officer, you'd have a mutiny on your hands before you could say "Bligh and the *Bounty*".'

A few days after Tuck had beaten me, Richard came running up with momentous news.

'They've caught the thief! It's Joshua Leverick, one of the starboard forecastle men. Caught him red-handed!'

'What's going to happen to him?' I said.

'I dread to think,' said Richard, and he was off.

We found out soon enough. The whole crew were summoned on deck to watch Leverick run the gauntlet. All thirty or so of the forecastle men lined up facing each other. Each carried a length of frayed rope, with the loose ends tied in little knots. In among the line were Lewis Tuck and another bosun's mate, each carrying a cat-o'-nine-tails. When Joshua was brought out on deck, with a marine clutching him tight by the arm on either side, he looked terrified. Unlike some men who faced punishment, there was no pretence of courage or contempt. Another bosun's mate ripped his shirt from his back with sadistic relish. At this moment I began to suspect that all the bosun's mates were as loathsome as Lewis Tuck. Every last one of them seemed to enjoy the cruelty in their work.

The bosun's mate who had ripped off Joshua's shirt

took a cutlass from his belt and held it, at arm's length, to his chest. At first I thought they were going to kill him, but Silas told me it was to stop him running down the line too quickly. Then, on the command of the Captain, the two of them – mate and victim – began to walk slowly down this row of men. As the punishment began, the whole crew, and especially the men in the line, started to jeer and hiss like a crowd booing a pantomime villain. The mate walked so slowly that each man in the line landed several heavy blows before Joshua was able to move on. When he passed the first bosun's mate with the cat, I winced as it cracked on his back. This was a blow too many. He collapsed, and the jeering line waited for him to recover and stagger to his feet.

By now Joshua could hardly stand. His face was contorted in pain, his body was covered in cruel weals, and his chest was bleeding from cuts inflicted by the mate's cutlass. He staggered towards the end of the line, but quailed when he saw Lewis Tuck waiting for him with another cat. That blow was the final one. He fell down on the deck, and did not move. 'Throw a bucket over him,' commanded the bosun. Joshua was drenched with stinging saltwater. This did not stir him, so a second bucket quickly followed. His hands began to clench and he tried to stand. Two men came forward and carried him off.

Ben turned to me and said, 'He's off to see Dr

Claybourne. His punishment's not over yet. Claybourne's got to put vinegar to them wounds to stop them festering.' All of us near to Ben – Tom, Silas, James – we all winced with mock sympathy.

It was a vicious beating and we had all behaved like a crowd at a Roman circus. Joshua seemed to be a conduit for all the anger and resentment and frustration the crew had kept bottled up during the voyage. Afterwards, when the men had dispersed, I felt guilty about being so callous, but there was something about being in an angry crowd that made it difficult to act differently.

A week later Joshua Leverick threw himself over-board and drowned. When a man died at sea, the crew usually auctioned off his clothes and possessions, and the money raised was sent back to the man's family. Not for Joshua, they didn't. He had broken a sacred rule. Seamen in a Navy ship have so little to protect them from the cruelty of the world, they depend on each other for help. Any man who broke that trust provoked a truly awful vengeance.

The evening after, I was sitting with Richard and Tom Shepherd in the mess. They began to talk, in hushed tones, of a book they had both read. It was called *The Rights of Man*, by someone called Tom Paine. Their discussion filled me with unease, as it seemed quite treasonous and certainly disrespectful of our king.

Tom went on to tell Richard about a reverend called Richard Price, and his Newington Green chapel, of which Tom used to be a member. 'He's dead now, bless his soul,' said Tom, 'but he changed my way of looking at the world.'

Tom and the reverend held views which shocked me, especially their support of the French Revolution. To me, and everyone else in Wroxham, the revolutionaries were worse than a pack of wolves. Instruments of Satan, the Reverend Chatham had called them, especially when they rolled out their guillotines and began to execute all the French nobles. We in the village all believed the rich man at his castle and poor man at his gate were part of God's preordained world.

But when I listened to Tom, who spoke in such a quiet, reasonable way, I couldn't help but think some of his ideas were undoubtedly true. 'The Reverend Price is a man of God too, Sam, so how can he be preaching the work of the Devil?' I had to agree. 'If a king is a bad ruler, then he doesn't deserve to be king. Have you studied your history, Sam?' I had to admit I hadn't, much. I could recite the English kings back to William the First, but I didn't really know much about them.

Soon afterwards, Tom gave me a beaten-up-looking book, which he kept hidden among the supplies in the hold. It was the very same book: Tom Paine's *The Rights of Man*. 'He's from your part of the world, Sam. Born in

Norfolk, but moved to Philadelphia. I hear he lives in France now. I picked this up in New York, on my last trip,' he said, 'so take good care of it.'

Then he began to explain, in an excited whisper, what the book was about. 'Paine says we shouldn't be ruled by people just because they're aristocrats. Being the son of a king or a duke don't make you any more fit to rule a country than being the son of a coal miner or a mill worker. True, they've got an education, these people. But we should all have education. Everyone should be able to vote, men and women. Then we'd be able to vote for Members of Parliament who would support ordinary people, instead of that lot now in the House of Commons, who are just looking after themselves. And what do we need the House of Lords for? They're all fat and old, and drunk on port for most of the time.'

I was horrified. I didn't want to offend Tom, but I knew enough about what he was saying to know this was treasonous talk. Didn't this man Paine live in France, after all? Besides, I barely understood what Tom was talking about. Parliament, the House of Lords, the House of Commons, these were words I had heard but little understood. I stared at him, almost speechless, while he talked. I took his book out of politeness, hurriedly placing it inside my shirt.

'Keep it to yourself, mind,' he said.

Later, at the end of the afternoon, when we were resting before the evening watch, I sat down in a corner of the forecastle, took it out and began to read. Engrossed as I was, I did not notice Lewis Tuck creeping up behind me.

'Got your nose in a book again, clever-clogs,' he sneered. 'And what's this you're reading?'

I knew he could not read himself, but still my mind went blank. I opened my mouth to speak, but could think of nothing to say.

Tuck seized on my discomfort.

'Seditious, is it? Treasonable material intent on undermining the morale of His Majesty's Navy?' He thwacked me round the head with his rope. 'Well, that's a floggable offence, lad. I think I'll have that,' and he snatched the book from my hand.

Help came from an unexpected quarter. Lieutenant Middlewych had been observing the whole incident. He came closer and spoke in an angry whisper.

'Leave the lad alone, Mr Tuck. Being able to read is not a punishable offence.'

Tuck sprang to attention. 'Yes, sir, at once, sir.' He tossed the book back to me and went on his way, giving me a look of seething rage that told me exactly what to expect the next time he caught me alone.

'Carry on, Witchall, carry on,' said Middlewych. 'Too few of our ratings can read. You should be congratulated.'

By now I had turned bright red, and my hands were

sweating so much I feared the book would slip from my fingers. Please God, I thought, don't make him ask me what I'm reading.

'What is it you're reading?' said Middlewych.

A thought flashed into my head. My maker had not completely deserted me.

'It's Captain William Bligh's account of the *Bounty* mutiny, sir. And his extraordinary fifty-day voyage across the Pacific Ocean to Kupang Harbour, on Timor Island, sir.' I began to gabble. 'The men on the little boat, sir, they had to eat raw seagull – beaks, feet and all, sir.'

'Good lad,' he said. 'Did you know Mr Nisbit was a member of Captain Bligh's crew? I'm sure he'll be able to vouch for the authenticity of the account. I'd be curious to read that myself. Perhaps you'd be good enough to let me borrow it when you've finished?'

Without waiting for a reply he turned and walked back to the quarterdeck. It was a full five minutes before I stopped shaking enough to feel I could trust myself to stand up and walk away.

Down on the mess deck I bumped into Ben and told him what had happened. 'Sam,' he said, 'where did you get that book? You could be flogged for reading that.' He snatched it from me and went to find Tom Shepherd. He and Tom were good friends, but I could see them both having a quietly furious argument. Had the bosun's mates not been present, I didn't doubt that they would have come to blows.

I did feel angry with Tom, after that.

'Ben says you nearly got me flogged!' I said when I saw him next.

'Sam,' said Tom firmly, 'you're a bright lad. There are things I'd like to teach you about the world. That book's the best start I can think of.'

I forgave him soon enough, but I still thought about how close I came to having the cat lashed across my back.

CHAPTER 8

Storm

After ten weeks on the *Miranda* words and phrases that had at first puzzled me now slipped from my tongue as second nature. So, too, did the actions that went with them. In the rigging I knew my way around the stays and halyards, clewlines, buntlines and slablines. Among the sails I knew at once the clew garnets, peak, nock and leech. I knew a horse was a rope you stood on whilst working the sails. Presented with a loose rope I could fashion a Blackwall hitch or a Carrick bend without a second thought. At the guns the trunnion, quoin, cascable, worm and crows of iron were the stuff of everyday procedure. I knew, too, my waisters from my idlers, and that the physical hardships of kedging and warping, when the ship was stuck in still water near to the coast, were nothing compared to towing the ship with a barge when it could not make sail.

I had become familiar with almost every part of the *Miranda*. I had even been in the Captain's cabin, yet it was weeks into the voyage before I went into the officers' quarters, which we called the gunroom. Early one morning, I was ordered to help fetch provisions from the bread room – which was most easily entered via a hatchway on the floor there. This was an unsettling glimpse into another world.

The gunroom was abaft of the mess deck, where there were small cabins on either side. This was an area ordinary seamen rarely ventured into. There was a barrier of marines to pass through first – as they always sat and ate between us and the officers. So when I was called into the gunroom I was curious to know what lay beyond that wooden partition.

I saw at once a long table set with an elegant lace cloth, with silver cutlery, blue and white china, and candles to supplement the lanterns that swung from the low ceiling. Glass goblets were set by each place, and a crystal decanter full of red wine stood at the top of the table. At the other end of the table a couple of roast chicken lay gently steaming. As the aroma wafted into my nostrils I felt a great pang of homesickness. We always had chicken at Christmas, Easter and birthdays, and I suddenly longed to be sitting around our dining table with my family.

At either side of the gunroom was a row of small wooden cabins for the officers. As I waited by the hatch to the bread room I caught a glimpse into the one occupied by the lieutenant of the marines. His bright red jacket was laid out on his cot, which stretched the length of the cabin and was covered by an embroidered cream bedspread. I could also see a small writing table, and a basin. A carpet covered the wooden deck, and I glimpsed a portrait of a pretty-looking woman and two children on the wall. For me in my hammock, sleeping with an entire watch of men packed shoulder to shoulder above the tables on the mess deck, the lieutenant's cabin seemed like a little oasis of luxury, although the room was barely a third the size of my bedroom at home. What would I have given to have my own small space of tranquillity and privacy on this frantic floating rats' nest? Then, in an instant, the lieutenant swept into his room, and the door slammed shut. This snapped me out of my little daydream. I took an armful of biscuit and was gone.

A few days later, I was sent down to the gunners' store on the orlop deck in the hold, to fetch replacement parts for our gun carriage. I rarely visited this gloomy spot, save to collect my powder cartridges, but was fascinated by its nooks and crannies. Tiny doors led off from the platform to the after powder room, the bosun's stores, sailroom, and other storage places. Beyond, at the very stern of the ship, our supplies of biscuit sat going mouldy in the dark. I never got used to the overpowering smell down here, and had to stifle the urge to retch. As I waited for the gunner to produce the parts I needed, I overheard an urgently whispered conversation. Here on the orlop deck was where the junior midshipmen slept, and I could make out the young one whom Silas had annoyed by staring too long at him, in a heated exchange with Lieutenant Spencer.

'But, Uncle,' said the boy, 'you know I never wanted to go to sea.'

'Don't "Uncle" me, Neville,' said the Lieutenant sharply. 'Such persons as Uncles are nowhere to be found aboard His Majesty's vessels. Well, you're here now, and you'd better make the most of it. Your mother is expecting me to look after you, but I shan't be mollycoddling you. Your father would be livid if he could hear you fretting like this. You've got five generations of Navy officers to live up to, and I'm going to make your family proud of you even if I have to take the skin off your backside.

'Now, next time I order you to climb to the topgallant, I expect an instant response. "Aye, aye, sir" is the only acceptable reaction. Not a lily-livered "I can't". You are on this ship to learn how to command men. And you can do that properly only if you win their respect. You won't always have a bosun's mate to back you up – especially when you go into battle.'

The midshipman seemed to wilt under this tirade, backing towards the wooden panel that fenced in the orlop deck from the hold. It got worse.

'And another thing,' went on the Lieutenant, 'get rid of that disgusting fungus that's sprouting on your top lip. Next time I see you it had better be gone, otherwise you'll be spending a couple of hours tied to the mizzen-masthead.' With that, Spencer turned and headed back up on deck. He walked past me without a second glance, indifferent to whether I had heard him or not.

As soon as he had gone, the boy began to sob quietly. Then he recovered himself, dried his eyes with a hand-kerchief, and began to climb up the narrow ladder from the hold to the orlop deck. I slid into the shadows. I knew from bitter experience how losing face could mould a boy's behaviour. I did not want him to know I had seen him, and have him punish me for it.

Later that day I was commandeered by Lieutenant Spencer, along with three other men. 'Run to the topgal-lant, lads,' he ordered, 'and make sail.' The sail, at the very top of the mast, needed to be let out a few more feet. Then Spencer turned to his nephew, who was also passing by. 'Mr Neville, accompany these men to the topgallant, and see they carry out my instructions correctly.' I could see the fear in his eyes. 'Aye aye, Lieutenant,' he said. The four of us swung out on to the rigging and began the laborious climb up to the top. The midshipman followed, scrambling behind us.

I could tell from the way he clung on so desperately that Mr Neville was not used to being in the rigging. As I climbed I was struck by two possible courses of action. I could try to show him up and humiliate him – sweet revenge on an arrogant young officer. Or I could try to help him. As we climbed into the cloudy November sky, the sun came out, and I took this as a sign. I shall be good, I resolved. When we reached the fighting-top platform, I deliberately went through the lubber hole right by the mast, rather than swing over the side of the platform as most seamen did. This, I knew, would make the midshipman feel less of a fool when he went through the hole himself. Then, as we approached the top of the rigging, I let him catch up with me so he would not still be panting up to the topgallant long after the rest of us had arrived there.

I could tell how scared he was by the way he was trying not to look down. As he drew level with me I turned and repeated the advice Joseph had given to me up in the rigging: 'One hand for the Navy. One hand for yourself.'

I half expected a dirty look, but instead Neville gave me a grateful smile. 'Thank you, seaman,' he said. 'I'm not a regular visitor to this part of the ship.'

We understood each other at once. He knew I knew he was frightened half to death. I knew he was grateful for my help.

The sails were soon let out, and on the way down he seemed to move with much greater confidence. He even started to whistle a jaunty tune.

'And what's your name?' he enquired. 'Witchall? Thank you, Witchall, for your kind words.' Then he was off.

There are many things to fear on a ship, aside from the bosun's lash and death in battle. When you lie in your hammock, or spend an idle hour sitting in the sun, your thoughts can wander to any number of catastrophes – not least shipwreck. Most sailors, I discovered, cannot swim – though I could. Neither does the Navy feel it wise to teach them. They could, after all, put this new-found skill to use in escaping from the ship.

I was dreading the prospect of a winter storm. Fill a small glass of water from the village pump and you'll believe it has almost as little substance as air. But fill a bucket or pail and carry it a quarter mile, sloshing and spilling as you stagger, and you realise water is an unruly and weighty thing. Sea water even more so – with its complement of salt, sand, strands of seaweed and little wriggling creatures. You can tell that when you swim in it. A freshwater river lets you sink like a stone. The sea pushes you up a little. When I was small I used to stand on the beach and stare out at the slow lazy curve of the North Sea horizon, and imagine the power and weight of the sea. Even when it was calm and flat it still filled me with awe. It stretched out to eternity, and yet I could only see the surface. Below lay gradually darkening waters, infinite fathoms deep.

An angry sea is one of the most fiercesome sights in nature. I fear a storm almost as much as I fear battle.

Richard and I were scrubbing the deck in the early morning when we first became aware of an oncoming storm. While we worked, we thought up nicknames for members of the crew. He loved my name for the tattooed thug and his Biblical quotations – Vengeful Tattoos. The Captain we decided to call Lord Mandible, and Edmund Ackersley, whom Richard particularly disliked, was known as By 'Eckersley, after a phrase he often used. Dr Claybourne became Dr Claymore, and Lewis Tuck became Lousey Tucker.

While we talked I noticed the sky was especially dark and foreboding. Dawn came so slowly I wondered if it would ever get light. Up in the heavens, clouds scudded across the sky at high speed, and the wind blew both warm and cold. Tossed to and fro by the wind, flurries of snow bustled around the ship, a touch of white against the grey sea and grey horizon. Icy spray from the churning sea hit me in the face. I shivered in my meagre clothes and wondered what manner of weather these strange atmospherics would bring.

We'd had some bad weather coming down the Channel, but nothing a sailor would write home about.

'I saw some storms in the *Franklyn*,' I said to Richard, 'but I've never seen anything like this before.'

'You joined the *Miranda* at a bad time of year,' said Richard. 'At the turn of the seasons, you often get rough weather.'

As the waves grew higher, Lieutenant Middlewych ordered the ship to prepare for the worst. Captain Mandeville was summoned to the quarterdeck. He looked especially haughty on that day – pacing around, flinty-eyed, barking commands at anyone who approached. All hatches were tightly sealed and the topmen raced aloft, to take down most of the yards and furl the remaining sails before the wind grew too high. Only the foretopgallant stayed lowered, to offer the ship some control against the coming tempest.

Surveying the sky again, I began to feel mightily afraid. As Ben passed he said, 'These ships are built to weather anything. The only thing that'll sink a frigate in a storm is the shore. If we were near shore, I'd be an anxious man.'

Later that day the helmsmen were ordered to lie to – to point the ship diagonally into the rising sea, to blunt the ferocious onslaught of the waves. The ship was lashed by the rain, which poured over us in sheets, drenching any man who ventured out in it. I thought I had my sea legs, but after a day of this, I began to feel desperately ill. In a flat panic I ran to the side of the ship to vomit, only to have it thrown back in my face by the wind. The stale, acrid stench clung to my hair and shirt until the rain slowly washed it away. All the new men on the ship were floored with seasickness. They looked as pale as spectres. Even the old sea dogs began to complain.

'It's fish we ought to be, not sailors,' said Ben. 'Still, no matter. We're safe enough away from the shore.'

'Not for much longer, we ain't,' said Silas. 'That's a north-easterly wind – it'll drive us on to the coast in no time.'

At mealtimes we stopped receiving warm food and drink. After an entire day of cheese, grog and ship's biscuits I said, 'You'd think they'd give us something hot on a lousy cold day like this.'

Ben shook his head. He was not in a good mood and his patience was paper-thin. 'Now, why d'you think we don't have anything hot to shovel down our throats?

Come on, Sam. You're supposed to be a bright lad.'

I shook my head.

'Captain's forbidden the cook to use the galley, hasn't he?' said Ben. 'Y' can't have a fire with the ship lurching around like this. Fire and storm. It's a devilish combination.'

The others warmed to this alarming topic. James chugged half his mug of grog and held forth. 'A fire can touch off the magazine, and blow everyone to slivers and fragments. If y' ship's on fire y' have to choose between getting burned to death in the flames, or freezing and drowning in the sea.'

So, drained by seasickness, soaked by the cold sea, weak, listless and shaky, we could only shiver in the mess deck. All we had to distract us was our turn on the daily rota at the ship's pumps – churning the winches around, baling out water for an hour a time. By the third day, the pump alone was not sufficient, and we were commanded to form a human chain to pass buckets from the hold. After a dreadful, dreary afternoon of this, we were sent back to the mess deck, and I began to wonder when our torment would end.

On the fourth day Ben told me the storm was driving us towards the coast of northern Spain.

'Looks like Silas was right. So much for me thinking we were safe out at sea. We've drifted a hell of a way,' he said. 'The coast's mostly flat and sandy beaches round these parts, but in weather like this even a harmless-looking beach can still wreck a ship. If we get caught on a sandbank off shore, the waves'll smash the *Miranda* to pieces just as sure as a jagged cliff.'

Soon after, one of the bosun's mates came down to the mess deck. He picked a handful of us at random, including Joseph and me, to go on deck to make more sail. Almost all hands were expected to man the sails whenever necessary, so it was no use protesting I was only a powder monkey.

The moment I came out on to the quarterdeck I began to fear for my life. I had never been ordered to go up the rigging in such bad weather. Rain poured down and winds buffeted all on deck to and fro. Lightning flashed across the sky, followed by the threatening rumble of thunder. No sooner had I walked out into the teeth of the gale than a great wave swept me over like a giant hand, so cold I thought it would stop my heart. Then, as it drained back to the sea in a bubbling torrent through the quarterdeck gun ports, it dragged me with it in its clammy grip, as surely as the tentacle of a giant octopus. Joseph rushed to grab hold of me, otherwise I would certainly have been swept into the swirling cauldron below.

As I staggered to my feet, I was aware that Lieutenant Middlewych was yelling in my face.

'Up the foremast, Witchall. You too, Neil. We need to set the topgallant.'

I could see a few of the foretopmen already clawing their way up the rigging, fighting every inch of the way. Joseph and I looked at each other, and put a reassuring hand on each other's shoulders.

We both swung out on to the rigging, and began climbing. At once my soaking clothes hung heavy on my arms and legs and made me feel sluggish. Then my teeth started to chatter uncontrollably, and my whole body began to shiver. For a moment, I had to stop to try and bring this shivering under control, lest I fall. Joseph noticed I was in difficulty and he grabbed my arm.

'You go first, Sam,' he shouted. 'I'll be right behind you.'

The topgallant was the highest sail on the foremast, and by the time I was halfway up the rigging I could sense my fingers going numb with the cold. Joseph and I reached the topgallant together, and the midshipman up there sent us either side to join men already stretched out to the end of both sides of the yardarm. There we waited for a few short moments, while other men clambered up the rigging to take up the remaining places. Hanging on for dear life from this vantage point, I could see the raging sea all around us. It was a sight not meant for humans. Below me, the waves formed heaving ridges. Then the horizon would drop, as the *Miranda* ploughed into a trough, and terrifying peaks would loom almost to the height of our yardarm. I felt like I was caught up in a green, living mountain that was trying to devour us.

Those with me in this precarious perch looked so terrified I was sure they thought their last moments had come. One man stared unblinking, straight ahead, his jaw clenched tight in fear and desperation. Another had wrapped his hands around the rope that ran across the top of the sail and then clenched them together in prayer. He was muttering a series of orisons which I could not hear. I looked down the yard to see if I could spot Joseph. He was there, three men down on the starboard side of the mast, hanging on with grim determination. He looked over to me too, with soaking hair plastered down his face, and laughed wildly. That was just like him – to make a jest out of our perilous condition.

Then, a sudden flash of lightning crashed over our heads, turning the grey-green world into black and white. We were all startled and momentarily blinded, but Joseph more than any of us. He lost his footing. When I looked again, I saw him hanging by one hand on the rope that ran beneath the yardarm – his body dangling into the void. The other men on that side of the yard were all swaying precariously – trying to steady their feet on the same rope.

'Help me up, y' useless lummox,' he shouted to the

man next to him. The fellow was too petrified to move, and just clung tighter to the top of the yard.

'Help him, you lousy bastards!' I screamed. At that point I think I was more frightened than Joseph.

Joseph reached up and managed to get both hands on the rope. I began to think he was going to save himself. Then he swung his body up to wrap his feet around the rope. The ship lurched alarmingly as it rode another wave, and his frozen hands lost their grip. With a chilling scream he dropped like a stone to the deck. There he lay in a crumpled heap. Utterly still.

The rest of my time up the mast I cannot remember. I suppose we must have let down the sail, then climbed down to the deck. I returned to the mess in a stupor, changed into my second set of clothes, and found a corner to curl up in.

Seeing Joseph alive one instant, and dead the next, I couldn't believe it. One minute he could feel the wind on his face and the rain on his back, smell the salty sea air, laugh, smile and curse; the next his life was snatched away from him. Limbs that would take him from the deck to the topgallant yard in barely a minute and a half would never move again.

That night around the mess table, talk turned to the final thoughts of a dying man. What went through Joseph's mind in that final few seconds of his life? Ben, who had quite a sentimental streak, said it would be his final farewell to his father, or a last warm hug from his mother before he went off to sea. I kept quiet. I wanted to say this was nonsense. Joseph's mind would be filled with livid terror, as his arms flailed desperately to catch hold of the rigging as it shot past at ever-increasing speed. I hope he didn't think, in those last seconds, of everything he was losing when he left this world.

'At least a fall is quick,' said Ben, trying to comfort me.

Edmund Ackersley put his tuppence worth in too. 'Fall's the quickest way to go, I reckon. Even them that's torn in half by chain shot takes a few moments to die. Scream and flail like a scalded cat, they do . . .'

Ben gave him a dirty look. 'Yer a cheery sod, Edmund. The lad doesn't need that sort of talk right now, y' misery.'

Poor Joseph. What a bright spark he was. I had a life. He didn't.

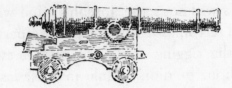

CHAPTER 9

The Cat and a Cat

In the weeks after the storm we patrolled the seas off northern Spain before heading south close to the coast of Portugal. The voyage settled down into a dull series of days, then weeks, when very little seemed to happen. No enemy ships were sighted, no remarkable weather blighted our passage, and the crew grew weary and sullen.

I learned to avoid Lewis Tuck as much as I could, and when this was impossible, I made every effort not to incur his wrath. Michael Trellis and his cronies would still issue their occasional taunts, but they knew I had friends who would protect me if their bullying edged into violence.

By mid-December we rounded the south-western tip of Spain and arrived at the Gulf of Cadiz. We were expected to reach Gibraltar a few days before Christmas. When ship's gossip about our nearness to Gibraltar reached Silas at the mess table, his eyes lit up. He told us, in a mischievous whisper, that last time he had served with the Navy he had spent some time in the hospital in Gibraltar, on account of a broken leg incurred whilst loading provisions. Despite his injury it was, he said with a smirk, a most splendid stay. For the nurses that staffed the hospital were almost all ladies of easy virtue, who were more than willing to perform all manner of lascivious acts in exchange for a few shillings.

'Every last one of 'em a dark-eyed beauty!' he said. 'Mind you, they all liked a drink too. A couple of them changed my dressing when they were three sheets to the wind. I had to drink a bottle of rum myself to deaden the pain.'

Seeing how the men around the table reacted to this titbit was a picture to behold. Some had eyes out on stalks, others shifted uncomfortably in their seats. Peter Winchelsea, one of the foretopmen sitting down the table from us, was blushing furiously.

'Oh aye, Mr Winchelsea, have you stayed at Gibraltar Navy Hospital too?' said Silas rather unkindly. Peter was well known as a pious man.

'I have not, sir,' snapped the foretopman, who was referred to as 'The Reverend' by his messmates. 'I am perturbed by your indecent observations. If I should have the misfortune to ever find myself in that hospital, I shall pray to the Lord to give me strength to resist these unholy sirens.'

Silas would not be drawn into an argument. Instead, he lifted his mug of grog, and said, 'A toast to unholy sirens. Long may they give us all manner of unmentionable diseases!' Most of us thought this a fine end to the conversation. Toast duly drunk, we went back to our duties.

The whole incident tickled Richard considerably, and when we were alone together on the upper deck he performed a splendid mime of everyone's reactions.

'I was wondering how I could get myself into the hospital too,' I confided. 'D'you think you could arrange it? Nothing life-threatening, or permanently disfiguring, though.'

'I'd go for a sprained ankle, myself,' said Richard. 'Or maybe a mild case of scurvy. Not enough to lose any teeth, but enough to make you go off-colour, and develop a few rashes.'

Ben told me about scurvy when I had been reluctant to eat a wormy apple. It seemed to eat a man away from the inside. Teeth fell out, gums bled constantly, sores and rashes covered the body, and any victim of the disease felt unutterably weary. It was preventable, for some reason, if a sailor ate fresh fruit and vegetables. And when these were not available, as I'd heard Dr Claybourne say, he should drink lemon juice. This was horrible, unless you mixed it with rum and water.

Richard and I hatched a plot to see if we could develop scurvy. But then we decided that these fabled ladies, especially ones we might be tempted to go astray with, wouldn't find us attractive with half our teeth dropping out. Besides, deliberately making yourself unfit for duty was a floggable offence.

'It'll have to be a broken leg, then,' said Richard.

'Perhaps we ought to take a leaf out of the Reverend Winchelsea's book after all,' I sighed. The subject was laid to rest.

Gibraltar loomed out of the mist three days later. It was strange for me, at a time of the year so near Christmas, to be in a mild climate. The few days before we reached the port were splendid – clear skies and calm sea, with a gentle breeze. For this brief period I actually began to enjoy being aboard the *Miranda*. Whenever I did feel sorry for myself, I'd think of Midshipman Neville, who had curbed his temper a great deal since the early days of the voyage, but who still looked rather lost and lonely, whenever I set eyes on him.

After I'd been up the foremast with him, he'd ignored me the next few times I saw him. But a few weeks later, when the ship had been off the northern coast of Spain and he was taking a navigational sighting with a sextant at noon, he'd called me over and explained what he was doing. Over the next few weeks a friendship of sorts had seemed to develop between us. Ben, ear attuned as usual to ship's gossip, told me his name was Robert and that Lieutenant Spencer was his mother's brother. The Nevilles, as I had suspected from his dress, were a very wealthy family.

'He's not a bad lad to have on your side, is Mr Neville,' said Ben.

Silas was less forgiving. 'Sucking up to the officers, eh, Sam?' he sneered, when he had seen us talking together. I could understand his resentment, although I still felt hurt by that remark. I liked Robert Neville despite of who he was, not because of it.

For most of the voyage, land had either been out of sight or some distant misty cliff almost indistinguishable from a cloudy horizon. It was too far away to imagine it as solid ground that did not sway beneath your feet, with trees and green grass, and friendly people. On the *Franklyn* I had never been away from land for more than a week, and this voyage had already lasted over three months.

As we grew nearer 'the Rock', as Gibraltar was known, I feasted my eyes on its contours and crags. The port had been built around a great rocky outcrop that thrust high into the air, and was visible a good twenty miles before we reached it. The rock was covered in lush green vegetation, and as we approched I could make out the government buildings around the port. Great fortifications snaked up the side of the rock, giving it a formidable air. Ben told me we had held on to this bit of Spain for nearly a hundred years. It was a useful place to have as a port.

On the morning we were due to arrive, Captain Mandeville summoned us all into the waist. 'We shall be arriving at Gibraltar this afternoon, and staying for two days whilst the ship takes on provisions and engages in minor repairs. The port is well known for its changeable climate and lively southern winds, so we shall keep to our sea watches. I shall also require you to assemble at eleven o'clock tomorrow, to witness punishment. Finally, no one on board, not even myself, will be going ashore. Marines will be posted on every exit point, with orders to shoot any man who attempts to leave the ship. That is all.'

With that, the Captain turned tail and vanished below deck. The bosun bawled, 'Ship's company dismiss,' and we hurried back to our duties. That dinner-time we wondered about who was to be punished and why.

Knowing that something awful was to happen the next morning cast a gloomy mood over the crew, and rather spoiled the pleasure we felt arriving at Gibraltar.

Later that day we moored in the harbour, and began the task of unloading empty food and water barrels and hauling fresh supplies aboard. Every one of us was looking forward to fresh water, fresh vegetables, fresh anything, really – aside perhaps from the poor wretch who was to be punished. Maybe he was too sick with anxiety to contemplate eating at all? I could not help but think about him, as one of the bosun's mates spent most of the afternoon sitting on deck fashioning a cat-o'-nine-tails in full view of us all, carefully knotting each of the nine strands before placing this wretched device in a red baize bag.

We spent the whole of the rest of the day reprovisioning – loading barrels of salted beef and pork, cheese and flour, bread, spirits and beer, biscuit, pease and tobacco. All of it was hauled aboard in the hot sunshine, and stowed away in the hold. There were even a couple of boxes of lemons. Dr Claybourne would be pleased to know that Mandeville wasn't so mean with his crew's health after all.

The next day fresh supplies of tar were taken on board, and heated up. We all set to work caulking the planking on the decks to make them watertight, with me being especially cautious not to spill any. A team of shipwrights from the port also came aboard to mend some leaks in the hold. By eleven that morning the smell of tar was overwhelming. Then the bosun's pipes were sounded, and he called out, 'All hands on deck to witness punishment.'

We all gathered around the mainmast, and the marines assembled in a bright red wall on the quarterdeck facing us, muskets held straight before them, bayonets attached. The ship's officers, all dressed in full ceremonial uniform, joined them. In front of them, a grating had been set up in readiness for the man about to be flogged. Standing next to it was one of the bosun's mates, clutching the red baize bag. It seemed shameful to be called upon to witness this cruel ritual on such a beautiful day.

When we were all assembled, two more marines appeared from below deck, dragging a man who was so terrified he could barely walk. I saw at once that it was Robert Hartley – one of Captain Mandeville's servants – and my stomach turned over. He was a slight fellow, with a timid manner at the best of times, and I could not imagine him bearing up well to such hard physical punishment. I wondered what on earth he had done to merit such an ordeal.

All was ready. Then Captain Mandeville appeared on the quarterdeck, and fixed us with a stern eye. He carried a copy of the Articles of War and began to read from Article 2.

'All flag officers, and all persons in or belonging to His Majesty's ships or vessels of war, being guilty of profane oaths, cursings, execrations, drunkenness, uncleanness, or other scandalous actions, in derogation of God's honour, and corruption of good manners, shall incur such punishment as a court martial shall think fit to impose, and as the nature and degree of their offence shall deserve.'

A brief silence followed, while we all wondered what possible derogation of God's honour and corruption of good manners mousy old Hartley could have been responsible for. Then Mandeville spoke again.

'Steward's mate Robert Hartley has been found guilty of stealing from the Captain's wine supply. The sentence is thirty-six lashes. Seize him up.'

With that Hartley had the shirt ripped from his back, and was spreadeagled face forward to the grating, his wrists and ankles tied with canvas. Meanwhile we all looked at each other with amazement, and asked ourselves in what moment of lunacy a man like Hartley would consider stealing from his own captain. It was the stupidity of it. And being an officer's servant was one of the easiest jobs on the ship. I wondered what Hartley would do if he survived. He was one of the most lubberly-looking men on the *Miranda*. I couldn't imagine him hauling up a mainsail or manhandling a gun.

The marine drummer boy beat out a tattoo. The bosun's mate took the cat from out of the bag.

An awful silence lay heavy over the ship, as the bosun's mate removed his jacket and braced himself to begin the whipping. The rope whistled through the air and landed with a hefty thwack on Hartley's narrow back. He let out a piercing scream, then again, and again . . . After twelve lashes Lewis Tuck came forward to take over the flogging. Another bosun's mate replaced him after his dozen strokes.

When it was over, Hartley's back looked as if it had been roasted in an oven. He was unconscious and had to be dragged below deck to the sick bay. It had been like watching a mouse being tormented by a pack of savage dogs.

At breakfast Ben told me Hartley had died during the night. 'Some men can stand to be lashed a hundred times, even two hundred, if they're the sort of brutes who're used to harsh punishment,' he muttered. 'But some men can't stand even a couple of dozen lashes . . .'

I felt sick at heart for the rest of the morning. My mood only lifted at dinner when Ben told us all that a consignment of mail had been delivered to the ship, and was soon to be distributed. Perhaps there would be news from home for me, and even a letter from Rosie?

My messmates all looked thrilled by this opportunity

to receive post. All except Edmund Ackersley.

'Don't get too excited,' he cautioned. 'Handing out of post on a Navy ship is always an anxious moment. For some, it's news of tragedy – wife or sister who's died having a baby, or a parent popped their clogs . . .'

Tom and James both shouted him down. 'Shut up, you dreary misery – y' like a death at a birthday party!'

But Edmund was in full flow. 'Worst of all is the death of a child. By 'eck, I've seen grown men collapse ont' floor and bawl their hearts out when news o' that reaches them.'

My excitement began to evaporate.

That afternoon we gathered around the bosun, whose job it was to hand out the post. Thanks to Edmund I just felt jittery – like we were drawing straws to decide who was to be flogged.

When the bosun called out my name I rushed to the front of the crowd and he handed over five letters. Two were from my father, and I read them quickly. He'd had a toothache, and had his tooth removed by a frail seventy-year-old called Mr Eade, who always pulled teeth in the village . . . and our two pigs had got drunk when a broken beer cask had been left outside our garden. They had snorted and slurped at the stream that leaked out, and had got so befuddled they could barely stand up . . .

The other three letters were from Rosie, which I kept

until a private moment when I could read them at leisure. I was not disappointed. Two had been written to me whilst I served in the *Franklyn*, and had been sent on. The first, written soon after I had gone to sea, was quite polite and formal. The second, a reply to a letter from me just before I was pressed, was much warmer. The third, written a week or so after she received news of my pressing, was a delight. She had drenched the envelope in rose water, although by the time it arrived this had turned to a faint, sickly-sour tang. I read this one over and over, smiling at her jokes, and feeling breathless and excited by her flirtatiousness.

In one passage she wrote:

Papa took me to Norwich last week, and as we walked through the market I spotted a dark-haired boy in the distance who I was sure was you. Of course I ran over, wanting to throw my arms around you, and when I caught up and grabbed the arm of this lad, he turned round with a look of complete surprise on his face. I was so sad, and felt such a fool when I realised it wasn't you.

When we got home that evening, I went for a long walk on my own down by the seashore. I wished that you were there with me, but my fairy godmother didn't answer me. I've obviously not been quite as good a girl as I ought to be.

She signed off with a heartfelt plea for me to look after myself:

If any of those Frenchmen attack your ship, head for the hold, and stay there until it's all over. Tell your captain I said it was all right to do it. Don't be a hero. I've no use for a dead hero. Come back to me soon,
Your dear friend
Rosie xxxxx

I folded up the letter and placed it in my shirt pocket next to my heart. This will be my keepsake and lucky charm, I thought. As long as I don't lose it, it will keep me from danger and see me through until we return to England. I reread it so many times it became frayed around the creases, and soon I could recall every word when I lay in my hammock at night.

Although I was beginning to think that Captain Mandeville was not quite as much of an ogre as I had first thought, I still made every effort to keep as far away from him as my lowly position allowed. Haughty, aloof and with a face perpetually hovering on the brink of a sneer or a scowl, he was clearly a man who had no need to be loved by either his officers or men. I would guess his age was perhaps thirty, and his wiry, bushy hair was already beginning to recede around the temples. I suppose his thin, pointed nose would be judged by some to make him quite handsome, but for me, it just added to his air of disdain. He was the most intimidating man I had ever met. Ruthless determination seemed to seep out of him like static electricity.

So I was horrified when I was summoned to Lieutenant Middlewych and told that the Captain had decreed I was to wait on his table that day. 'Captain's a man down, Witchall, after that business with Hartley. All you have to do is bring food to the table, and take it away when you're asked. Most of the time you have to stand very still, right at the back of the cabin, and pretend you're part of the furniture.'

Seeing me looking so anxious, the Lieutenant gave a brisk smile. 'Don't worry. You won't be on the menu. Buckley will be helping out too. He's done it before and he'll tell you what to do.'

Richard, I discovered, had already been briefed. Mandeville was entertaining the Governor of Gibraltar Sir George Beverly, an admiral with a civil post, who still had an active interest and influence in naval affairs. Beverly was bringing his wife, and his three daughters. Also present would be the frigate's three lieutenants. A pig from the ship's manger had been slaughtered that morning, and the Captain's cook was busy preparing it. Even as we spoke, the sweet smell of roasting pork wafted by. It was mouth-watering, and I'm sure it tormented the whole crew, whose daily nourishment was much the same as the pig's.

Richard had a conspiratorial air about him, and he leaned close to tell me, 'Gossip has it that Mandeville has a sweet spot for one of the Admiral's daughters. Miss Beverly, I believe. She's the eldest. We don't know whether it's a real sweet spot, or whether he thinks it'll get him another promotion.

'Look and learn, Sam. See how Mandeville tries to solicit the Admiral's favour. But watch out. The people you'll see tonight will regard you with the same indifference as they would a sparrow come to perch at their window.

'Hey! One last thing,' he said. 'Don't catch my eye, or I'll start to giggle. If we both start they'll tie us by the wrist to a barrel hoop, and have us flog each other on the backsides.'

The hours before the meal crawled, and Ben and Tom seemed most amused by the ordeal I was facing. I was summoned by the Captain's steward just before one o'clock and he told me to change into fresh clothing and wash.

'We have some fine young ladies coming aboard,' he told me. 'We've got to look presentable.'

I returned, as instructed, at half past two, and was directed into the Captain's cabin. Like the officers' gunroom, the Great Cabin was another world. The long mahogany table had been covered with a linen cloth and the tabletop gleamed with silver cutlery, candlesticks and cut-glass goblets.

The Admiral and his family arrived at the quayside just after three o'clock. Piped aboard by the bosun, who saluted with great dignity, they were ushered to the Captain's cabin. Richard and I were standing smartly to attention at the back of the cabin, ready to be summoned when we were needed. The rest of the Captain's guests were all wearing their most formal uniform – cleaned and polished to perfection. As they waited, Mandeville's lieutenants seemed uneasy in his company, but had the social grace to pass the time making small talk about the weather. Mandeville seemed his supremely confident self, and I was amazed how a man could flog to death a servant one day and entertain with such assurance the next.

I was grateful to Richard for the talk we'd had earlier. What I heard that afternoon was quite extraordinary. In Norfolk those of a higher station, such as the Reverend Chatham, or the gentleman farmers with estates close to the village, had behaved with courtesy to their congregation or labourers. Although they took their own higher station for granted, they made it clear that they had responsibilities too. The people who dined with Captain Mandeville were cut from a different cloth.

The Admiral entered first – a great tall fellow, who seemed to stoop even in the high ceiling of the cabin. He was stout too – obviously fond of beef and Burgundy. He seemed to have a matter-of-fact air about him, which was to contrast quite noticeably with the haughty opinions of his wife and daughters. The Admiral's wife, Lady Beverly, swept in immediately after, and all attention turned to her. She was a small, thin woman – undoubtedly pretty, but with a sour, impatient look on her face.

Then the three daughters came into the cabin. Each looked quite dazzling, in long, high-waist dresses, with silk shawls draped around their shoulders. Introduced by their father from eldest to youngest, as Miss Beverly, Miss Louisa and Miss Anne, they all curtsied and smiled primly at the lieutenants. Miss Beverly was tall, like her father, but was as slender as her mother. Louisa was shorter and quite buxom, Anne was a slip of a girl, around my own age.

Miss Beverly carried a small basket, out of which popped a tiny ginger and white cat, barely out of kittenhood. This, she announced, was a gift from her family to the Captain.

'His name is Bouncer, and he comes from a very fine line of ratters.'

Bouncer took one look at Mandeville and hissed, which made me like him immediately.

'He's a game little puss,' said the Captain, but I could tell he and Bouncer were not going to be friends. 'Back in his box with him,' he said, 'we'll find him a berth later!'

I stood there, silent and still as a statue, watching with a detached fascination. It was Miss Beverly who captivated Mandeville and his lieutenants. And me too. She had a wonderful halo of curly brown hair, held with a red-silk ribbon that matched her dress. Her hair was cut to above her shoulder, all the better to show off her slender neck. Had her face been perhaps a little less broad, and her eyes a little larger, she would have been exquisite. But she was pretty, though, and graceful in her manner and movement. Her younger sister Louisa was the real beauty of the family – she had skin as smooth and white as alabaster, which set off her white muslin dress. Her pale grey eyes had long dark lashes, and her hair was black as the night sky. But Louisa seemed to lack Miss Beverly's natural grace. She laughed too loudly, and ate with too great enthusiasm. Her mother gave her the occasional flinty-eyed glance of disapproval, and she would compose herself rather obviously. Still, the two young lieutenants either side of her seemed desperately eager to engage her in conversation. Anne was seated opposite her mother and had her back to me. I wondered if this was her first grown-up party.

Watching them, I realised how much I longed to talk

to a girl, to spend some time in female company. I enjoyed the companionship I'd found at sea, but now I was part of a world where beautiful young women were alien visitors. Seeing the lieutenants fawning away, it occurred to me that they were enjoying the novelty as well. They too were uneasy with the gentle sex.

With the ring of a bell, the Captain's steward announced the soup course. Richard and I sprang into action. Standing close to both Miss Beverly and Lady Beverly, I became aware of the perfume they wore. A flowery scent – rich and intoxicating, and miles away from the tar, stale sweat and sulphur that usually filled my nostrils on the *Miranda*. As I leaned over Miss Beverly to collect her empty plate, I noticed too the freckles and down on her bare, slender arms, and the soft swelling of her breast in the low neckline of her dress. Even though I had cleaned myself up, I felt like a homeless beggar, with three months of dirt and sweat seeped into my skin.

I noted, when I placed the soup dishes before the dinner guests, how only the Admiral made any acknowledgement of my presence, and that was just an amiable nod. To the other visitors I might as well have been invisible. It was exactly how Richard had predicted. And as evening fell, and the wine flowed, their table talk began to astound me.

Most of the conversation was about London 'society'.

When they said, 'The whole of London is talking about it,' they meant, of course, the very select few – and by implication, the people they knew.

Then Lady Beverly, I suspect in an attempt to rile either her husband or the Captain, said, 'I hear that some of our captains are entertaining the notion that tea should be given to the lower deck' – by that she meant ordinary seamen – 'instead of their grog or Scotch Coffee.'

'That is indeed the case, Lady Beverly,' said Mandeville, with as much grace as I ever heard him talk to anyone. He certainly was out to impress tonight.

'But,' said Lady Beverly, 'tea is well known for its refining properties. Surely, such a degree of refinement would be incompatible with the character and calling of our seamen?'

'Quite so, ma'am,' replied the Captain. 'Which is why I rarely supply my crew with it. Refinement is not a virtue in the human material from which our Navy is formed. Our Jack Tars need to be as hard as granite. If they were made of less stern stuff, then the empire we command would not be ours for much longer.'

'Refinement!' The Admiral snorted. He clearly thought this conversation was ridiculous. 'There's no danger of refinement in the men of the lower deck. A greater set of rascals you'd never meet. Most are, in truth, the sweepings of our gaols. Most of them mix their words and oaths in near-equal proportion, unless they've the stern eye of a bosun's mate overlooking them. If you see them on land, they commonly indulge in drunkenness and foul language, and render themselves easy prey to the harpies that wait in all our ports. And yet,' here the Admiral really got into his stride, perhaps wishing to make amends for these observations for those of us present he was so roundly abusing, 'our gallant sons of the waves have stood fast against the united powers of Europe. These bold fighting fellows are buffeted by the oceans day in and day out, they are baked alive in Antigua, or turned to icicles in Hudson Bay. Yet there's rarely a ship where the captain would say there was not a man or officer among his crew he'd wish to change.'

'Hurrah, hurrah,' went the lieutenants – the toadies – and raised their glasses.

Then conversation turned to America where, Lady Beverly lamented, there was 'a most disgusting equality'. She went on to condemn the Americans as traitors fit only to be hung, drawn and quartered. Here Miss Beverly piped up, complaining of 'the barbarous use of English'.

'I hear they call any wide street an avenue,' she continued, 'regardless of whether there are trees either side of it or not. Cousin Henry has recently returned from New England, and was pained by how rarely one hears a sentence correctly pronounced.'

I looked over at Richard, hoping to find a glint of amusement in his eye. But I saw only cold contempt. I'm glad I did. If he had been stifling a laugh, I too might have joined him.

But then, rather to my surprise, Captain Mandeville drew this conversation to an end by remarking that he had served with several Americans, and indeed several were even among his crew today, and that they were all fine men.

'Despite our recent difficulties,' he said, 'America and Britain still have close ties and even warm feelings towards one another.'

Dislike him as I did, I admired him for having the courage to voice a clearly unpopular opinion, and for some small defence of my friend.

His words were well chosen. 'Quite so, Mandeville, quite so,' said the Admiral firmly. His wife shrugged in a non-committal way and Miss Beverly blushed a little, perhaps wondering if she had incurred her father's displeasure.

Talk swiftly turned to lighter matters. When the party finished the Admiral and his girls were escorted away with much ceremony. I watched them go, and wondered when I would ever see any three girls as lovely as those.

After the guests had gone Richard and I helped the

Captain's other servants to clear away the table and prepare the cabin for the next day. Mandeville returned. He took us two boys to one side, and gave us each a shilling.

'You did well, lads,' he said. 'You may yet have the honour of waiting on my guests again.' Then he went over to the cat basket, which had been placed by the window. 'Witchall, take responsibility for this. I can't stand the wretched things myself. But look after it well. If Miss Beverly visits again, I'd like her to know that "Bounder" here is thriving.'

I was surprised that Mandeville had remembered my name, although he had already half forgotten the cat's. I felt embarrassed by this sudden geniality, and hurriedly saluted and scurried away. Bouncer, no doubt taken from his mother only the day before, mewled pitifully in his basket. The cook came over and called me into the galley. A saucer of milk was produced, and then a few scraps of pork. The cook slipped a few slivers over to me too, with a quick wink, and I wolfed them down. I had not tasted meat as good as this since I left home.

I crept back to the mess deck and placed Bouncer and his basket under my hammock. But he kept up a lonely meowing and other men, sleeping nearby, began to complain. I plucked him out, and he snuggled up next to me – warm and purring. Having him there in my hammock brought me some contentment, and I fell asleep almost at once.

That night I dreamed of home. I was sitting by the fire. Outside, dusk was falling over snow-covered fields. Light from the fading sun bathed the scene in a pink glow, casting long shadows over the hedgerows. Pepper, our family cat, was sitting by the window sill, meowing to be let out. I felt safe and warm and snug, until the day began with the bosun's cry of 'OUT OR DOWN'.

When I woke, the cat was no longer there, although he had left a small damp patch on my bedding. I found him lurking around the galley. Word quickly got round the men that the *Miranda* had acquired a ship's cat, and that I was entrusted with its care. The cat adjusted to life aboard the boat well enough. The cook would feed him scraps, and I dare say his diet was as good as ours. Every so often Bouncer would go missing, and I would spend an anxious half hour scouring the ship. Being responsible for the cat was a mixed blessing. If any harm should come to him, I was sure Captain Mandeville would hold me responsible. Some of the crew sensed my concern, and told me lurid tales about what happened to the ship's previous cat.

'Took him to the hold, to get rid of the rats, and nothing more was 'eard of him,' said Edmund Ackersley. ''Cept they found a bit of his tail among the ballast.'

'That Bouncer's a fine-looking cat,' said Tom Shepherd, 'but I don't like having them aboard. I was on a coastal trader a few years back, sailing out of London. There was a cat on that – MacTavish he was called. Big black hairy thing with green eyes. Belonged to the cook. Always scurrying round the galley, begging for scraps. One day, when we were docked at Whitby, a coal from the oven dropped out and landed right on his back.'

'Poor old thing.' I winced.

'Cat shot into the air,' Tom went on, 'screeched like a mad thing, then shot off down into the hold with its back on fire. Went straight into a cargo of hemp, which went up like a tinder box. That we could have dealt with, only there were twenty-odd barrels of gunpowder right next to it. We all ran off that ship as fast as we could. It blew half the quayside to pieces. Funny thing is, the cat survived. He came out from under the hemp, still blazing, then blundered straight into the bilgewater in the keel. That put him out, and he ran up the stairs straight off the ship. The cook was distraught. He cared more about where the cat was than what had happened to the ship.'

Bouncer soon grew out of his little basket. The carpenter made him a larger one so he could nest among the sheep and goats in the pens in the upper deck. Sometimes he slept there, among his fellow creatures, and sometimes he snuggled up with me. In truth, he didn't live up to his boisterous name, or his reputation as a ratter. Bouncer was a soft and friendly cat, and small for a Tom. Many of the crew doted on him, giving him an affection they could not lavish on their absent wives or children. Small he may have been, but he grew quite portly on all the scraps he was given.

Many of the more superstitious members of the crew were sure the cat could sense the restless spirits said to haunt the ship. Sometimes, especially at night, Bouncer would stop dead, and his tail would bristle and shoot up. He'd hiss and spit, then back away. Richard was convinced he'd seen a rat. I wasn't so sure . . .

'I like this cat,' I said to Richard when Bouncer leaped up to sit on my lap. 'But I don't like having to be responsible for him. Mandeville would have my guts for garters if anything happened to him.'

'No fear, Sam. I have a brilliant idea,' said Richard. 'We need an understudy in case he meets an untimely end. What we need is a lady cat, and a set of kittens. We can pick the one that's most like his dad, and keep him hidden away. If Bouncer goes over the side, or gets eaten by the rats, we'll just substitute the other one. I'll bet the Captain, and his lady friend, if she ever comes back, won't notice the difference.'

'Richard,' I said, 'how on earth are we going to find a lady cat in the middle of the Gulf of Cadiz?'

'He'll have to make do with a catfish,' said Richard. 'Maybe Ben's mermaids will have one as a pet.'

CHAPTER 10

To Quarters

As we sailed up the Portuguese and Spanish coast on our journey home, the talk around the mess table and forecastle was mainly about battle. If and when it would come, who we would fight, how quickly we would overwhelm our enemy, how much prize money we'd make. Most of all, the men liked to boast about how they had fought in previous battles. Down on the mess deck, among our gun crew and on neighbouring tables, I overheard far more than I wanted to know about the awful reality of hand-to-hand combat.

'And I crept up behind him and cracked his napper with my musket butt . . .'

'I dodged that knife he threw down from the fighting top, and felled him with my pistol . . .'

'Just as we drew alongside, I threw down a grenade and it landed in a group of French marines, and killed five of them . . .'

James Kettleby was more wary. 'The French and Spanish carry more men and marines aboard their ships,' he told me. 'That's why we try to kill as many of them as possible before we get to boarding. They, in turn, try to destroy our rigging so we can't manoeuvre the ship. Then they can board us and crush us.'

None of this helped to ease my fear of boarding.

When talk turned to battle I always kept quiet. Ben noticed my silence. When we were alone he said, 'They like to brag, don't they? A good battle gives a chappie the chance to show his mates what he's made of. Don't you worry, Sam. I'll look after you. And besides . . . us Tars have a well-deserved reputation. When we meet Johnny Dago or Johnny Frog, you can bet your life he'll be more frightened of us than we are of him. I'm not frightened of battle, lad. So you shouldn't be either. It's what we've been training so hard for over the whole of this voyage. And if things get bad, just remember "The hotter the battle, the sooner the peace".'

Richard was keen to avoid a scrap too, but he

understood why the men were keen to fight. 'I'd be quite happy never to see a single Spanish or French ship, believe me. But for this lot, it's a bit of variety. Still, if we ever do get dragged into a fight there's always the prospect of prize money – that's something to look forward to.'

Every morning I woke fearful that the day would be the one in which we'd meet an enemy ship. At every dusk I felt a bitter-sweet twinge of anxiety. Today I survived, I'd tell myself, but tomorrow . . .? Several of my messmates reassured me most frigate patrols passed without incident, but I just knew in my bones that the *Miranda* was not going to be so lucky.

Eventually it happened.

'Sail ho!' We all heard the cry from the lookout at the main mast. A shiver went through me. It was half an hour before noon, on a bright January morning. We were just off Cape Ortegal, on the northern tip of Spain. A ship was coming up from the coast and heading straight for us.

Soon after we heard that warning cry, the bosun's whistle summoned the whole crew on deck. The Captain, surrounded by his lieutenants and a squad of marines, was waiting to address us from the quarter-deck. We gathered around the mainmast, waist rail and up the rigging, each of us straining to hear the Captain speak. He looked excited. In fact, he looked rather pleased with himself.

'Men. A Spanish frigate is approaching us from starboard, no doubt keen to claim us as a prize. I intend to meet her head on in battle. The Spanish sailor is poorly trained and poorly led, and I'm confident that by the end of the day we shall all be drinking a victory toast. Meanwhile, I estimate our foe will be upon us within an hour or so, which leaves enough time for a good dinner. You shall all have an extra ration of rum today. I should like to remind you that the British Tar is unbeatable in battle. Nevertheless, according to the Articles of War, the penalty for desertion of post, refusal to obey an order, and open cowardice, is death. But I'm sure you will do me proud today.'

With that, the men burst into a loud cheer. Then they began to sing the battle song 'Hearts of Oak'.

Hearts of oak are our ships,
Jolly tars are our men,
We always are ready,
Steady, boys, steady,
We'll fight and we'll conquer again and again.

It is an extraordinary thing to hear two hundred and fifty men singing at the top of their voices. Despite my fear, it filled me with euphoria. Even Richard, who was by my side, joined in. When we were alone together he would quietly scoff at displays of British patriotism. But not today. 'When in Rome . . .' he whispered to me between lines, and winked.

We headed for the mess deck and sat down at our usual table. The atmosphere was certainly lively. I looked around the mess at my friends and comrades, stuffing their faces and talking excitedly with their mouths full. I wondered how many of them would live to see the coming evening, and how many gaps there would be in the benches the next time we all sat down to eat.

'Now then, Sam,' said Ben. 'No gloomy thoughts.'

Richard chided me. 'You should feel lucky. You're down on the gun deck, safe behind your wooden walls and big gun. I'm up in the mizzenmast with a musket – plain as daylight for anyone to pick off!'

'You sound remarkably cheerful about it,' I managed to say.

My messmates were in a fine good humour, but I could barely eat. My mouth was so dry every mouthful of dinner seemed like a cold stone in my throat. I had to force myself to concentrate on what was being said to me. From that moment the lookout issued his warning, with everything I did I wondered if I would be doing it for the last time. I thought fleetingly of Mother, Father, Tom and Rosie. What were they doing now that death was staring me in the face? Peeling potatoes, buying tea in Norwich, picking mussels from the rocks?

The Spanish frigate was making slow progress – sailing up to meet us against the wind. We ate our meal with no great sense of urgency. I began to regain confidence when I downed my ration of grog. My fear receded, and I felt a brief surge of pride. Ben was right. These men were magnificent. They would give our Spanish foes a good hiding.

By the time we were called to quarters by the marine drummer boy my fear had returned, but I was trying hard to keep it well hidden. I bid Richard a hearty farewell, and put out my hand. He ignored it, and gave me a bear hug instead.

'See you later . . .' he said with a grin. But I could tell he was frightened too and trying hard not to show it.

We were called to quarters every day – it was a tedious drill that had always irked me. But now I could see our months of practice had been worth the effort. It took us barely more than five minutes to prepare the *Miranda* for action. Every man and boy on board knew exactly what he had to do, but this time the significance of what we were doing struck me hard. While some of us hurriedly carried the Captain's furniture and the ship's remaining livestock to the safety of the hold, others soaked the decks, then scattered wet sand around to stop us from slipping on any blood that was bound to be spilt.

The crews cast loose the guns and opened the gun ports. I ran as fast as I could to the ship's after magazine, to collect my gunpowder. On the way I heard the angry sizzle of water on hot coals as the galley fire was extinguished. On the orlop deck Dr Claybourne would be laying out his horrible implements, saws and forceps and all, to treat any wounded man brought down to him.

When we had crossed the French corvette close to the start of the voyage, it had never felt like we were going to fight. But this, I knew, was going to be the real thing.

Our preparations completed, we waited at our stations. I don't know whether it was because my heart was thumping so hard in my chest, but in those long minutes before action I saw everything with a crystal-clear clarity. I stood behind my gun, watching dust whirl in a thin, bright shaft of sunlight which poured in through a vent in the deck. Ben stood before me in a striped shirt. Next to him was Tom, calm as anything. Surrounding the gun were James and Silas, Oliver and Edmund. Each wore a determined look. Coiled, ready to spring into action. Two of them had taken their shirts off, in anticipation of the hot, sweaty work to come. All of them wore a strip of cloth tied around their forehead and over their ears, to keep the sweat from their eyes and deaden the roar of the guns.

As the seconds ticked away we waited at our posts, every muscle tense, wondering at the significance of every command we heard shouted out on the quarter-deck above us. We knew the enemy were approaching from the shore, and I kept hoping for a glimpse through the open gun port. But until action began we did not know which side of the ship would fire first. Perhaps we would be called over to assist the starboard gun crews. I hoped not. I had faith in my crew. I wanted us to be firing our gun, and them assisting.

As the Spanish ship drew closer, several of the topmen were called away from the guns. Then we heard Lieutenant Middlewych call out a series of commands concerning the setting of the sails.

'Mandeville is trying to get astern of the Spaniard,' whispered Tom. 'If we can rake her, we'll have won the battle from the start.'

If a frigate could get in front of or behind the enemy, she could pour devastating fire right through the length of the ship. If the Spanish crew were as poorly trained and led as we hoped they were, we had a good chance of doing this.

There on the gun deck, waiting for action to commence, we lived in a world of sound. Our view of the outside was restricted by what we could glimpse from our gun port, and what we could deduce from the noises we heard. So we listened hard to Middlewych call out his commands. Apart from his instructions, the ship was silent. Although we occasionally whispered to each other, most of what I heard was the creaking of the rigging, or the rattle of the ropes of the tiller as the men on the wheel swung the rudder to try to get us in the best position to fire our guns.

They say men in the pit of fear soil themselves. I never understood that. Inside me every bit of my stomach and gut just tensed up fast into some cramped uncomfortable ball. My fingers clutched so tightly to my cartridge box I wondered how I might ever let go . . .

When I had long ceased to expect it, I heard two loud explosions rolled across the sea. An instant later, there were two great splashes of water either side of our bow. Instinctively I reached to touch Rosie's letter in my shirt pocket. 'Keep me safe, keep me safe,' I whispered to myself. A rumble of muted voices swept through the ship. I heard Silas say, 'She's firing her bow chasers,' before Lieutenant Spencer shouted us all back to silence.

So, our opponent was now in range, although she had already wasted her opening salvo. We too had a pair of guns in the bow, and Spencer issued the order, 'Bow chasers, fire when ready.'

We waited in tense anticipation. Then, after a minute, both our bow guns were discharged. One shot brought a splash of water, the other a rending crunch of metal on wood. The crew gave a triumphant cheer and Spencer yelled, 'Steady, boys, steady. Bow chasers, fire when your target presents. The rest of you, await your orders.'

'First blood to us,' whispered Ben. I sensed a growing excitement among the crew.

We heard another loud bang, and a terrifying crash. The air was immediately rent with screaming from a couple of badly injured men. I hardly dared look, yet could not help a glance up to the bow. A cannonball had blown one of our bow chasers off its carriage. Fortunately for the rest of us, the gun had blocked the enemy shot, and it had carried no further along the deck. One of the gun crew, horribly injured, was turfed over-board. Another was swiftly carried to the forward hatchway by four of his companions, and down to Dr Claybourne.

The First Lieutenant called out, 'Port your helm . . . steady!' and we could sense the ship slow down and turn in the water. 'Steady! Standby larboard guns. Prepare to fire when target in sight . . .'

Oliver Macintosh, nearest to the gun port, caught a glimpse of the enemy frigate. 'She's got her stern to us. We're all set to rake her.'

It was a perfect manoeuvre. Mandeville had succeed-ed in getting the *Miranda* behind his foe.

'Larboard guns. Fire when ready!' yelled Spencer. As

the *Miranda* sailed on, each of us, from the bow to the stern, unleashed our shot. At intervals of a few seconds, five cannon fired before us. Every shot but one hit home with a violent crash. I waited for our turn with an unholy eagerness. As the frigate came into view I could see the damage we had done. Most of the windows in the Captain's cabin were smashed, giving the stern the appearance of jagged teeth in a gaping mouth. I saw, too, that the vessel was called *La Flora*. Then, Ben yelled, 'Make ready!' – the signal for all of us to stand clear of our gun before firing.

He pulled the trigger lanyard for the gunlock and the gun lurched back with a huge roar. I could not see whether our shot hit home, as smoke immediately obscured the view through the gun port. Neither could I hear, as the discharge of our gun had set my ears ringing. But I imagined our shot ripping through the gun deck of the ship, leaving carnage and chaos in its wake. Four shots had gone before it, carving great chunks from the insides of *La Flora*.

Through the smoke and the singing in my ears I suddenly became aware that Ben was yelling at me. 'Powder, Number Twelve. Jump to it!' I took the top from my cartridge box, pulled out a cartridge and handed it to Tom. As the rest of the crew loaded the gun for the next salvo, I ran as fast as my legs would carry me to the after magazine. Ahead of me, waiting by the wet curtain for his next cartridge, was another powder boy. It was Michael Trellis. He looked as white as a sheet, and had a purple bruise on his forehead.

'What happened to you?' I said. The boy said nothing, but instead of hostility I saw only shame. The marine guarding the powder room spoke harshly.

'Tried to run and hide in the orlop deck, didn't he! Mr Neville walloped him with a pistol butt to send him back up here.' The marine turned directly to Trellis. 'You're damned lucky Mr Neville didn't shoot you dead, son. I would have done.'

I disliked Trellis too much to feel sorry for him, but I could not despise him for his actions. He was nearer to the bow gun than me, so he must have seen the effect of the enemy shot in sickening detail. I decided to say nothing more to him, and nodded grimly. I could still hear muffled screams, though, from the orlop deck. Whoever had been brought down there was howling like a banshee. Above us, to add to the noise, four more of the larboard gun deck guns fired their shot, along with the guns and carronades on the quarterdeck above them.

When I ran back with my cartridge box, I immediately noticed how much hotter it had become on the gun deck. All around was frantic activity. Every gun was at various stages of reloading. Barrels were being swabbed, burning fragments hooked out, cartridges and cannonballs loaded, and wads rammed home. I had been gone barely sixty seconds, and already our crew were needing my cartridge, which was snatched from my hand the moment I returned.

'You need to be quicker than that, Sam,' scolded Ben. I could only just hear him. 'We've been waiting a good ten seconds for this.' I shot off again for the next one, not wanting a further telling off.

On the way down into the ship my hearing returned, and I heard the First Lieutenant call, 'Brace up the weather yards' – further orders for the topmen to turn the *Miranda* around, so that the crews on the starboard side could discharge their guns. Moving swiftly within a lurching ship is very disorientating – especially when you have no way of seeing outside to determine your bearings. I returned to the gun deck, and needed to check where my crew were, in case I rushed to the wrong side of the ship.

Within a couple of minutes the *Miranda* was sailing back across the stern of our opponent. One by one our starboard guns began to splutter out their deadly load. Once again my ears began to ring, and although I could see Ben or Tom shouting orders to me, I could not hear what they said. I felt grateful for those endless afternoons of gun drill. I knew exactly what to do, and exactly where to stand.

Again, the First Lieutenant called out to the topmen

to adjust the sails, and again we turned to allow the larboard guns to bear.

'I'll wager we're closing in to board,' said Ben.

'So soon,' I said, with more apprehension than I meant to show. After such a long wait for action to begin, I never expected things would be moving so fast.

Sure enough, the *Miranda* began to edge towards *La Flora*. 'Larboard side. Prepare to fire,' shouted Spencer. 'Guns one to five reload with chain shot and aim at the rigging. Guns six to ten load with grapeshot and aim at the upper deck.'

As we grew level with *La Flora* I could see she was in distress. Only one of the gun deck guns was still firing. Others poked out of their gun ports at odd angles, or not at all. From two ports towards the stern, smoke poured out. I caught a glimpse of angry yellow flame in the inside of the ship. Our raking broadsides had wreaked terrible destruction. But the quarterdeck was not badly damaged, and as we grew closer, the guns began to fire.

Again, the gun crews on *La Flora* let her down. The first three shots fell wide, causing great fountains of water to shoot up in front of our bow. But others hit home. One shot slammed into the foremast with a sickening splinter, and I heard something – almost certainly one of the yards – crash on to the deck. Further sounds of splintering and crashing followed. I heard a man scream, and a bosun call for help. I prayed it wasn't Richard that was hurt, and all at once I felt mortally afraid.

The next shot from *La Flora* landed near us, showering our crew with dust, tar and debris. A hole appeared in the deck timbers close above us, and one of the mizzentopmen lay sprawled across the gap, his head and arms dangling down. I looked into his face and could see at once he was dead. A steady stream of blood began to pour down one of his arms, collecting on his outstretched fingers, and dripping down on us. The poor man was grabbed by a couple of unseen hands, and pitched over the side. If this was not enough of an indignity, they lugged him over right by our gun, so his lifeless body crumpled into the neck of our gun, before sliding off and into the deep.

An instant later, *La Flora* came within scope of our gun. 'Make ready!' We fired. As soon as I had delivered my cartridge for the next shot I hurtled below for another. By the time I returned, the crew had already fired again, and were waiting for me. Ben clasped an encouraging hand on my shoulder, and so we continued as the *Miranda* edged closer to her quarry. Our gun-fire was devastatingly effective. The Spanish broadside that had damaged our foremast and upper deck were among the last useful shots the enemy gunners discharged.

Through the ringing in my ears, and constant series of

explosions, I sensed the bosun's whistle. Then I heard the command: 'Prepare boarders.'

This was the moment I had been dreading. But now I felt only great excitement. *La Flora* was struggling terribly. We were winning, just as the men had said we would. I sprang to pick up a pistol and a cutlass from a rack placed in the centre of the gun deck, and charged on deck to await further orders. There was Richard, safe, thank God! It wasn't his yardarm that had fallen to the deck. He looked quite exhilarated, having watched the whole action from high in the mizzenmast.

Now I was out on deck it was possible to see just how much damage the *Miranda* had sustained. Our rigging was a shambles and shots had ripped many of our sails. Worst of all, our fore yardarm was lying across the forecastle and the foremast leaned giddily awry above the topsail yardarm.

But when I looked over to *La Flora*, she was in a more pitiful state. Sails were torn and drooping, and her yards and upper masts had crashed down on her deck. Just at that moment a loud explosion erupted near her bows, and thick black smoke billowed out. She was now on fire on the gun deck both fore and aft. We were close enough to see that the crew were in disarray. I could hear officers shouting orders, but no one was taking any notice. One officer tried to gain the attention of a cluster of men on the deck by drawing a pistol and firing it into the air. This had no effect so he fired his other pistol at one of the men. This worked, but not in the way he intended. Two of the men stepped forward, ran him through with daggers, and threw him over the side.

Mandeville called out, 'Hold your fire!' When the *Miranda* had lapsed into silence, he had Lieutenant Middlewych call over to *La Flora*, shouting with all his might through a speaking trumpet. Middlewych spoke a little of many languages, and I presume he asked the Spanish if they were prepared to surrender.

We were not expecting the response. There was a loud explosion. I nearly jumped out of my skin, and thought *La Flora* had begun firing at us again. But instead more smoke began to billow from her stern. It must have been another cartridge going off in the heat of the fire already raging on the gun deck.

At that moment I realised we would not be boarding *La Flora*. The crew we could see milling around the deck were in such a state because they knew first hand how badly she was burning.

'Hove to,' shouted Mandeville. 'This fellow is going to go up like a firework.'

As the *Miranda* drifted a safe distance away, we saw the crew abandon their ship. One of her boats was launched, but it was so overloaded that it sank soon after, its occupants clinging pathetically to the upturned hull. Two other boats packed almost to capsizing did get away, and began to pull for the distant shore.

As the fire began to eat into the belly of the ship, those left on board faced a dreadful decision. They could take their chances in the water, or perish in the coming inferno. By now the excitement of battle had begun to fade. I no longer felt elated or afraid. In fact I felt a twinge of sorrow for my Spanish foe. Over on *La Flora* men balanced on the deck rail crossed themselves before plunging into the chilly sea. On a warm day I would not have fancied their chances of getting to shore. But on this January afternoon the sea was cold enough to take the breath away, and chill the life out of a man in the water.

On the quarterdeck of *La Flora* we saw an extraordinary sight. The captain and his first lieutenant stood surveying their ship. I could see who they were by the distinctive scarlet plumes on their hats, and the scarlet trousers and waistcoats they wore. They were conversing with each other in a calm and measured manner, almost as if they were sipping coffee in a drawing room. They seemed determined to go down with their ship. I wondered what they could possibly be talking about.

It was only a matter of time before the fire got to one of *La Flora*'s magazines. The stern erupted in a bright white flash, sending shards of wood, canvas, the captain and his lieutenant, and most of *La Flora*'s few remaining crew, high into the air. We were far enough away from her to avoid any injury to our ship, but even so, we were peppered with some fragments. As the smoke cleared and debris settled, a greater flash tore the forward section of the ship asunder. This was the larger forward magazine, and the explosion broke the back of the ship. Within seconds both blazing bow and stern were pointing up to the sky, rigging and yards from the masts were horribly tangled, and *La Flora* was beginning her final voyage to the bottom of the sea.

There on the deck of the *Miranda*, we all stood transfixed by the spectacle – too awestruck to even cheer. The more seasoned among us were probably cursing their lost prize money.

Then, as the smoke from the rapidly sinking ship drifted over us, the bosun called out, 'Three cheers for Captain Mandeville!'

That seemed to break the spell. Action had not found us wanting. We had lain waste our opponent with skill and courage. We cheered for our captain, and cheered for our lives. We had faced down death and survived. I felt a savage rush of glee, found Richard and hugged him tight, the two of us leaping around in a two-headed, four-legged jig. We were alive! Alive!

Then, as the smoke thinned and the heat haze of the explosion settled into a shimmer, those of us who cared to look towards the coast could see the black outline of another ship right behind the tangled remains of *La Flora*. She was heading straight towards us.

Again, a man high in the mast called out, 'Sail ho!'

It seemed the day was repeating itself. Only this time we were exhausted from battle, had a badly damaged foremast, and dusk was fast approaching.

CHAPTER 11

Another Prize

All eyes turned to Mandeville. To my surprise he looked unruffled.

'Gentlemen, another prize awaits.'

This time there would be no long delay before combat. The enemy ship was much closer, and the wind had changed direction. They would be upon us within half an hour. In the brief lull between the fighting, topmen swarmed up the rigging to bind up the damaged foremast and the carpenter's crew hurriedly set about patching up the holes in the ship.

We had another problem. Although the pale winter

sun was still shining in an almost cloudless sky, the sea was growing choppy. A stiff breeze was blowing in from the north-west, and sea water was swilling in through the damaged bow. Some of it ran out through the vents in the strakes, but water was beginning to seep down to the hold. Mandeville called for the ship's pump to be constantly manned.

By now, in that late afternoon, the effect of the midday grog had worn off. I felt sick with both exhaustion and the horrible sights I had witnessed. The fear I felt at having to fight another frigate hung over me like a clammy thunderous sky. Perhaps the Captain sensed our mood, for we were quickly issued with another double dose of grog.

Before we returned to the gun deck, a few of us were picked at random to clear some of the debris scattered across the upper deck. I found myself grappling with a broken length of yardarm and Silas came to help me heave it over the side of the ship. Lewis Tuck was overseeing the work, and as we strained to lift the yard he hit me with his rope.

'Put your back into it, y' lubberly slug.' Maybe it was the grog that made me do it, but I was so shocked I let go of the yard and furiously turned towards him. Instantly I regretted it, for I had placed myself in danger of a flogging. But before I could turn back to my work he had seized me by my shirt and placed his face right next to mine. 'What?' he hissed.

Silas snapped too, and before I could stop him he pushed Tuck away from me. 'Leave that boy alone,' he said with cold anger.

Tuck lashed back with his rope. 'You two get back to work. I'll deal with you both when this is over.'

I could not believe it. Now, if we survived the coming battle, we both faced the almost certain prospect of a flogging. 'Silas,' I said, trying to stop myself from crying. 'Thank you for trying to help me, but aren't we both in terrible trouble now?'

Silas looked stunned, as if he too could not believe what had just happened. 'It's too late to worry about now, Sam,' he said. 'Whatever happens with Tuck isn't going to be half as bad as whatever's going to happen in the next hour or two.'

Before I went below I took a final look at our new enemy. She was larger than *La Flora*, to be sure, and I knew for certain she would prove to be a tougher opponent. Back at our guns we waited in that awful tense silence. We could hear the Captain and First Lieutenant issue increasingly bad-tempered commands to the topmen as they tried to manoeuvre the *Miranda* with her damaged sails.

Then we caught a glimpse of the approaching frigate on our larboard side. She would soon be near enough to fire her bow chasers. Perhaps she was waiting to get close enough for a really shattering broadside.

'Heave to,' shouted Mandeville, and presently the *Miranda* creaked and groaned as her sails strained against the wind to bring her to a halt. This was too much for our damaged masts and rigging, and we heard a grinding, cracking sound as rope and wood split asunder. Down on the gun deck we did not know for sure which masts or yards had fallen, but judging from the direction of the sound, it was the foremast. This would certainly hinder our ability to outmanoeuvre an enemy frigate.

Ben spoke for us all when he whispered, 'It's down to us now, boys. Let's make quick work of this.'

A bare minute later, the starboard gun crews were ordered to the larboard guns, and we were joined by the six men who worked opposite us. We had trained together almost every day, but they kept to themselves in the mess, and I barely knew them. Almost immediately, Lieutenant Spencer shouted, 'Fire!' We set off our guns in sequence along the deck, from bow to stern, as the *Miranda* passed along the course of the approaching frigate. The orderly sequence of gunshot gave me heart. Again, my ears immediately began to ring, as the noise on the gun deck was deafening. The enemy frigate returned fire too, and shots began to whistle between our rigging.

As I ran from the magazine with a new cartridge, the

crew were waiting for another clear shot. 'She's called the *Gerona*,' said Tom, who had caught a glimpse of her stern as she passed by. Although my hearing was returning I could still hardly make out what he said. Then, we waited. No shots came from either side, and only the creaking rigging and sloshing of the sea could be heard. We strained our ears to give us some clue as to the course of action. Spencer called for the starboard men to return to their guns, and for us all to fire when the enemy came on to our sights.

'Make every shot count, lads,' shouted the Lieutenant.

In the silence we heard a lieutenant order the quarter-deck gunners to move the two 6 pounders to the stern gun ports. My stomach turned over. This could only mean that the *Gerona* was trying to place herself behind us. We heard the exertions of the men above us, and the creaking and grinding of the gun carriage wheels against the deck. We understood from the angry shouting that moving the guns was a desperately urgent task.

As we waited, an awful air of expectation filled the gun deck. I glanced fearfully down the ship, and wondered how the men closest to the stern were feeling. If we were raked, they would be the first to suffer. Then we all heard a distant bang, followed a second later by horrible pandemonium. A shot from the *Gerona* came crashing through the starboard deck. I looked over to see the two aftermost guns mangled together – their crews crushed and dismembered. All at once an horrific screaming came from that quarter of the deck, before another shot whistled through on the starboard side. This one met nothing more solid than flesh and bone as it passed the length of the ship, before lodging near to the bowsprit. Men on the starboard side were torn in two, or had arms or legs plucked away by the speeding cannonball. Blood and worse began to cover the deck, and the doctor's men rushed to carry the less seriously wounded below. Those who had escaped the carnage had to gather up the remains of their dead and mortally injured friends and send them tumbling through the gun ports and into the sea, before their lifeblood and innards made the deck too slippery to work on.

God forgive me, but at that awful moment I thought, *It's them, not us. Let it keep being them. Please, God, don't let me be thrown over the sides with half my insides spilling out.*

Among the chaos, I became aware that our ship was again crossing the path of the *Gerona*. Spencer yelled, 'Larboard guns. Fire when ready!' and once again we started to set off our guns. As the *Gerona* came into view, and just before we fired off our shot, I noticed she was now close enough for us to see her crew on deck and in the rigging.

We closed in, side by side. Once again Spencer commanded the starboard gun crews to join the larboard men. The *Gerona* was firing steadily too, and we could hear parts of our masts and rigging crack and fall. Mandeville must have decided to slug it out, because from this moment on we kept getting closer and closer. Among the deafening noise and bright flashes, I ran back and forth to fetch powder while people mouthed words I could not hear. Amid the drifting smog and encroaching dusk, everything happened with a strange slowness or impossible haste. The gun deck became unbearably hot, and I was drenched in sweat. The smoke from our guns caught my parched throat and I ran to the water barrel to quench my thirst.

Hurrying between decks I began dreading the return to my station. I began to long for the moment when I could run below for another cartridge to the safety of the mess deck and magazine where enemy shot would be less likely to fall. As I emerged from the mess deck companionway and back on to the gun deck, I knew that death was waiting there for me.

Events began to merge into one swirling blur. Sometime during the action, I could not tell you when, rigging and canvas from the foremast fell over the gun ports of the forward guns, and the crews were immediately dispatched on deck to help clear the debris. As we closed in on the *Gerona*, their gun crews turned their fire away from our masts and sails and on to the hull. One shot crashed into the quarterdeck. Another shot landed on the gun deck near to the bow. At this point I sensed that our crew began to work even faster and with greater fury than even before. We were matched one to one against our opponents in a duel where rapid fire was the only thing that mattered. I stood by my gun, waiting for the wall to crumple before me, clutching the box of gunpowder. If anything hit it I would be blown to pieces. Then, this overwhelming terror would ebb away as soon as the cartridge was taken from my hand, and once again I had the blessed relief of rushing down to the magazine for a few moments' safety.

I returned to an utter shambles. While I was gone, the gun crew next to ours had been hit. Three men around the gun were sprawled in various positions, dead, unconscious or screaming. The boy who served that gun was lying dead on the deck. *Let it be them. Not me.* That was all I could think. Now I would have to take over his job and serve the surviving crew as well.

With two guns to fetch cartridges for, I could spend less time in the shooting gallery, and more below deck. As the battle continued, the deck by the after magazine filled with injured bodies. Some sat waiting, grimly patient – with splinters sticking from their arms or legs. Others, especially those who had lost limbs, writhed in mortal agony. The rules for the doctor's attentions were fair. Men were dealt with strictly in the order they arrived – with no favourable treatment for officers. On one trip to the magazine I glimpsed my friend Tom Nisbit, with a bloody red stain over his shirt. I had no time to speak to him, and he died soon after. He had been shot through the chest by one of the *Gerona*'s marksmen. He had survived Captain Bligh's *Bounty* mutiny, but not the *Miranda*.

Soon we were so close to the enemy that we could glimpse inside her gun deck, and see the silhouettes of men darting about their business. The closer we got, the more fearful I became that a gun crew on the *Gerona* would be able to blast a shot straight through our gun port. Our crew had been firing almost constantly for over half an hour, and must have felt quite spent. But still they laboured, toiling with their hot and heavy gun.

Ben could see a gun inside one of the *Gerona*'s gun ports right opposite ours, which would soon be pointing straight at us. 'They're just swabbing out for another shot,' he shouted. 'Quickly, lads, or we'll all be blown to kingdom come.'

I waited helplessly for Tom Shepherd to take the cartridge off me so I could go and get another. As I waited I checked in my shirt pocket. Rosie's letter was still there, but the envelope was damp with sweat and the ink of the address had begun to run on to my white shirt. 'Don't fail me, Rosie,' I mouthed to myself.

Then Tom shouted at me to hand over the cartridge. Quick as a flash I unscrewed the top of the cartridge box, whipped out the gunpowder and was gone. Down to the magazine I ran, feeling like the last few seconds of my life were ticking away. When I returned, our crew were just aligning their gun with stays, and Ben was calling for another quoin to lower the elevation.

'Quick, lads, quick,' fretted James Kettleby, sweat pouring down his grimy face in rivulets.

'Steady as she goes,' said Ben, who was working with an ice-cold determination. Through the hatch I could see the other gun crew trying to aim their gun. I could make out their gun captain placing a burning rope to the powder hole.

'They're going to fire!' I shouted.

Ben didn't flinch. Then he yelled, 'Make ready!' and pulled the cord on the flintlock. Our gun burst into life, and when the smoke cleared I could see our shot had sailed clean through the enemy gun port and knocked their gun right over. We yelled ourselves hoarse with delight. If we had been a second later, all of us would have been killed.

Just then, I was startled to hear the bosun's whistle calling for the boarders. In all the tumult of battle, I had forgotten this would almost certainly end with hand-to-hand fighting. Ben and I went at once to pick up a pistol and cutlass from the barrel behind us, and headed upward.

The stairway to the quarterdeck was almost

immediately forward of our gun, and I was glad I did not have to walk through the bloodbath on the gun deck to get to it. But as soon as I came out on deck, I could see an horrific panorama. Much of the foremast was gone – pitched over the side. The mainmast, too, had been badly damaged, and yardarms and canvas lay in splinters and tatters on the deck. In the confusion of battle I could not recall hearing this happen. Our carefully maintained rigging had been utterly destroyed. All around lay bodies. There were so many that I wondered that there must have been far more killed, and those remaining had not yet been thrown into the sea.

The number of men gathering on our deck to board the *Gerona* seemed worryingly small, although I was relieved to see Richard still among them. I grinned wildly when I saw him, but all he could manage was a tight-lipped smile. Other men, who had been fighting on the topmost deck throughout the battle, also looked grim. I sensed events were not going our way. Lieutenant Middlewych confirmed my fears.

'Men, prepare to repel boarders!'

It was us that were about to be boarded, not the other way round. A glimpse over the rail towards the *Gerona* revealed a much larger number of men on her deck. All were armed to the teeth and boiling with murderous intent. I also looked over to the quarterdeck. Captain Mandeville was lying on the deck, a bright red stain down the front of his white waistcoat. Two midshipmen were propping him up and getting ready to haul him down to the doctor.

Middlewych rallied us for the coming melee. 'Men, stand your ground. Carronades prepare to fire . . .'

We waited in fearful anticipation as musket shots from marksmen up in the *Gerona*'s rigging whistled between our ranks and over our heads. When the *Gerona* was about fifteen feet away two of our carronades fired a volley of grapeshot into the Spanish warship. The shot thudded violently into the deck rails and scythed through her crew. Splinters flew in all directions. We followed this up with a barrage of 'stinkpots' – hand missiles. One of these exploded in the hand of the man who lit it, blowing his hand off and killing the marine next to him. It was not a good omen.

When the smoke cleared from our grapeshot and stinkpots, the *Gerona* was a bare ten feet from us. There were fewer men standing on her deck, but I could be sure they still outnumbered us. She was slightly taller in the water, and looked menacingly over our upper deck. One bear-like man was standing on the rail swinging a grappling hook. Just as he let go, one of our marines shot him and he fell into the water. But his grappling hook lurched over, and landed with a splintering clunk on the deck. Others quickly followed. Soon the *Miranda* was caught tight in the *Gerona*'s grip.

Seconds later, the Spanish crew began to swarm aboard like a great human wave – over us, left and right of us . . . Almost at once, I found myself facing a tall, handsome Spaniard. I engaged, I parried, I lunged, but he was both bigger and stronger. As I backed away, Ben leaned over from nowhere, and ran him through. 'Gerroutofit!' he yelled in a fighting frenzy. It was the last thing he did. An instant later a Spanish sailor planted a boarding axe in his forehead. He dropped like a stone. I turned to face his attacker, only to find myself fighting a huge brute of a man. I had picked the most mismatched opponent. He seemed puzzled by my impudence, then lunged over to cut me down. I remembered I had a pistol at my waist, drew it and shot him at point-blank range. The expression on his face changed to startled surprise, then horror, as he fell to his knees.

After the first mad rush of combat, I looked around and saw that we were overwhelmed. Yet I dared not surrender, for fear of being accused of cowardice.

It was then I heard a whistle pipe and Middlewych shouting through the confusion. 'Men, we must strike. Throw down your arms.' It was not a moment too soon. Three Spaniards had surrounded me, each pointing a cutlass at my chest. I stood, cornered by the starboard rail, and prayed they would have the grace to let me live.

Some men, still locked in a frenzy of combat, fought until they were pulled apart. They continued shouting obscenities at each other until they were hustled behind their comrades. I stood there panting, exhausted but relieved to still be alive. Richard was there too, and Robert Neville. For the first time, I noticed a sharp pain in my left arm, and saw that my sleeve was covered in blood. I lifted the sticky fabric to look inside. There was a shallow cutlass slash near to my shoulder. I had been lucky.

The Spanish sailors stepped aside to let a tall, noble-looking fellow pass between them. We knew at once that this was the *Gerona*'s captain. He stepped forward, distinctive in his navy-blue and scarlet uniform, a bright feather plume waving to and fro atop his hat. I thought he looked rather gaudy compared to our captain in his splendid outfit.

Middlewych greeted him with dignity, and the two men spoke with admirable civility. 'Your men fought with great courage, Lieutenant,' I heard the Spanish captain say. Middlewych bowed his head, then handed over his sword.

The surrender ceremony over, we were quickly herded below decks. Those of us untouched by the battle or wounded and able to walk were placed to the rear of the gun deck, just outside the Captain's cabin. There we collapsed, exhausted.

Then it hit me like a boulder. Ben had been killed. My friend, my Sea Daddy. I had seen it, of course, but now it came back to me with awful clarity. So too did the moment when I had fired my pistol into the Spaniard who was trying to kill me. I had actually taken the life of another man . . .

I sat down on a bench, and wept. At a time like this it would be Ben who would come and put a comforting arm around me. Not any more. Richard came instead. He hugged me, and he cried too.

'That was so horrible,' he said over and over.

Middlewych came over to us and said, 'Pull yourselves together, boys,' but he didn't have the heart to be angry. The rear of the mess started to fill up with survivors of the battle. I noticed with some relief that Silas and the rest of my gun crew were still alive. The hand-to-hand fighting had been over so quickly they had not even been called from their posts to fight.

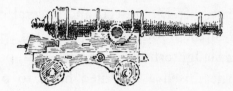

CHAPTER 12

Prisoners

As we gathered in the rear of the gun deck I tried to count the number of survivors, and reckoned on there being less than a hundred and fifty of us. That meant that a hundred or so men had been killed in the fight with the *Gerona*. What was to become of us? I wondered if the Spanish treated their prisoners as badly as the French were supposed to. Would they treat us worse, because they resented our presence in Gibraltar?

The rear of the gun deck became crowded. A Spanish lieutenant came and ordered some of us further down into the ship. We were herded on to the mess deck and the officers' gunroom was opened for us. Inside were Dr Claybourne, Mr McDowell and several of their assistants. All of them looked as if they had spent the afternoon in a slaughterhouse – which, I suppose, they had. Claybourne raised a bloodied hand to protest at this intrusion, but the Spanish officer just waved him away. He sighed and shook his head.

'Men, y'll just have tae give me plenty of space.'

Dr Claybourne had moved his surgery to the gunroom when the orlop deck became too crowded with dead and dying men. His most recent patients lay propped against the gunroom cabins – some not long dead, others in a desolate half-world between life and death.

Laid out on the table was Captain Mandeville. He was in a serious state – white as a sheet and unconscious. A musket shot had pierced his chest, and the doctor was now preparing to operate.

McDowell went over to the senior Spanish officer guarding us and talked to him in halting Spanish. The man nodded and called out an order to a marine. Shortly afterwards, Claybourne was presented with a fresh bowl of water, into which he rinsed several bloody cloths and sponges.

'Right,' he said. 'Now we'll begin.'

While we tried to keep a respectful distance,

Claybourne cut away the bloody clothing around Mandeville's chest. He proceeded to insert a finger, then a metal probe, into the wound. He turned to McDowell and asked him to have a look. I was amazed, under the circumstances, that Claybourne was still performing his role as teacher to his apprentice. Perhaps he knew already that Mandeville was a lost cause.

Claybourne spoke softly to McDowell. 'Chest wounds such as this, like yer head wound or belly wounds, they're ones for St Jude. If there were other men t' treat now, I'd leave him t' die in his own time. But we can still try.' So, while McDowell held the wound open with a clamp, Claybourne burrowed inside Mandeville's chest with a tweezer-like instrument. He pulled out a fragment. 'The musket ball's shattered inside him, y' see? It's all got to come out, or he'll not stand a chance.'

Claybourne called for more light, and two of his assistants held lanterns near to the Captain's chest. The burrowing continued. Every so often Claybourne would produce another fragment of metal and lay it carefully on the side of the table. I watched with a fearful fascination, and felt grateful that Mandeville was oblivious. I couldn't imagine how agonising such a procedure would be for a man who was conscious.

Five minutes later, Claybourne wiped a bloody hand over his brow and sat down. McDowell used some of the swabs from the murky water bowl to mop up the wound. Then two of the assistants raised Mandeville up so they could wrap a bandage around his chest. No one looked pleased with their work.

Activity over, we settled down for the night. A few wounded men whimpered softly, but by now most of those seriously hurt in the fighting had died and gone over the side of the ship. No one felt like talking. We just sat there, packed tight together, alone with our thoughts. My arm began to sting where I had been nicked by the cutlass. A year ago, back home in Wroxham, such a wound would have made me tearful. That night it seemed no more troublesome than the prick of a thistle.

An hour or so after the operation Captain Mandeville came round. Middlewych went over to see him. For a brief moment he seemed remarkably clear-headed, then he became delirious and began to ramble.

'So close to victory. So close . . . Just think, Middlewych. We could have sailed into Portsmouth with *La Flora* tied behind. The whole town would have turned out to welcome us. People would have climbed on to the roofs of their houses to see the spectacle. Cheering and waving . . . There would have been a knighthood for me, and a captain's commission for you. And glory enough to impress the Governor and beautiful Miss Beverly. What a pretty neck she has . . . And such exquisite manners . . . How fate toys with us. Now we'll be lucky if we don't get dismissed from the Navy.'

Middlewych seemed uncomfortable with this level of intimacy. 'Yes, sir', 'Indeed, sir', he would say at appropriate moments. If the circumstances had not been so grim, it would have been almost funny seeing Middlewych propping up this forbidding man, and trying to comfort him by making polite conversation.

As the night progressed Mandeville grew more delirious, and began to call for his mother. Then he began to have an imaginary conversation with his father. 'Don't go . . . stay with me. Don't leave me in this wretched school. Please, Father, please . . .'

Silas eyed him coldly and whispered, 'He'll not be with us by the morning.'

Mandeville started to ramble pitifully about the life he would never live to enjoy . . . the Admiralty post he aspired to, then perhaps a Member of Parliament. A manorhouse in Kent, full of little Mandevilles – the boys just like him, the girls as pretty and gracious as Miss Beverly.

Exactly when he died I could not say. His breathing dropped to almost nothing. Then his chest rose to take in a final gasp of air which passed out of him in one long sigh, like a ghost escaping through his open mouth. I never imagined I would feel sorry for the Captain, but his death was such a lonely one. Even though I was one of the lowliest creatures on the ship, I, at least, had my friends. If I had died down in the hold, I would have been surrounded by people who would have mourned me as a friend. Mandeville died hundreds of miles away from anyone who even remotely liked him.

Soon after, as we sat dozing in the stifling atmosphere of the lower deck, a Spanish officer made his way through the ranks of marines that stood guarding us. This man spoke to us in Spanish, and waited impatiently while his words were translated by another Spanish sailor.

'Gentlemens, half come to the *Gerona*, half stay here.'

Then these two men spoke to Middlewych. They conversed awkwardly, but eventually nodded in agreement. Middlewych spoke to us all. 'The Spanish are asking for men to man the pumps, as water continues to rise in the hold. We can work two at a time for half-hour shifts.' He turned to a bosun's mate and asked him to set up a rota.

His task completed, the Spanish officer nodded amiably, turned on his heels and left. When he'd gone Richard began to ape the accent of the sailor who had spoken to us. Silas was not amused.

'D'you speak Spanish then, Yankee-doodle-dandy? Not as good as he speaks English. Be thankful someone can speak to us in our own tongue.'

Richard looked suitably chided. I never knew with him whether he was genuinely sorry or just playing a part. Then Silas whispered, 'They're splitting us up because we could still have them. There's enough of us here to cause a lot of trouble. We could still get out of this pickle, and sail the *Miranda* back to England!'

Richard, my gun crew, Lieutenant Middlewych and perhaps another fifty of us remained in the *Miranda*. The rest were taken off to the *Gerona*. I saw that Michael Trellis was among them. The thought of several years in a Spanish prison with him for company was too much to bear. Then all of a sudden, I remembered the fight with Lewis Tuck and Silas and me just before we went into battle. I looked around quickly for Tuck, but could not see him.

'What happened to Tuck?' I whispered to Silas.

'Don't know, Sam,' he said. 'Let's hope the bastard's been killed.' He winked. I sighed with relief. That was one thing we did not have to worry about for now.

We stayed below deck for the rest of the day. Once again ours was an enclosed world, where we had to rely on our ears rather than our eyes to gather information. Throughout the morning we heard the dragging of wood on wood, and banging and shouting. Middlewych spoke a little Spanish. From what we could overhear we deduced that our captors were setting up a jury mast. Some other work was going on above our heads, as the damage done to Mandeville's cabin by those raking cannonballs was patched up.

Middlewych looked thoughtful, and spoke to one of the bosun's mates. 'I'm guessing that if they're jury rigging the ship, then we've a fair journey to make. If we were nearer a port they'd just tow us.'

Later that morning, a couple of Spanish marines came to take away Mandeville's body. For the next couple of minutes we made not a sound, listening hard to see what would happen. Then there was a splash, and we realised they had put him over the side of the ship without so much as a few prayers, let alone a funeral.

'Sic transit gloria mundi,' said Middlewych. I thought he was muttering a prayer, until Richard whispered in my ear.

'Thus passeth the glory of the world,' he said. 'It's Latin. Like "Tempus Fugit", and "Brutus aderat forte, Caesar adsum Jam". I don't think Middlewych liked the Captain very much.'

When you are feeling sorry for yourself there is nothing more hateful than the sound of other people laughing. We sat all day in the stifling, darkened gunroom, listening to these Spanish sailors jabbering away ten to the dozen in their mysterious language. As the evening drew on, they began to celebrate their victory. From what we could hear, many of them were getting raucously drunk. A plot began to form in Middlewych's mind. He spoke at length to Silas, and Silas came over to Richard and me. I knew before he'd even started to speak that there was trouble afoot.

'Good evening, lads,' he said with an ingratiating smile. 'The Lieutenant here has a plan which may result in us escaping from this mess.'

Richard and I looked uneasy. 'Does it involve us by any chance?' said Richard.

Silas smiled in a non-committal way. 'Come over and talk to the man,' he said.

Middlewych gave us one of his mirthless smiles. 'Witchall, Buckley. Listen to that!' We did . . . drunken singing filtered down the stairs from the gun deck. 'Most of them seem to be having a party, although I'd be a little more cautious myself if I had fifty Englishmen to keep an eye on.'

'We're not all English, sir,' said Richard, rather cheekily.

'Indeed, Buckley,' he said wearily. 'Now here's my plan. We need a couple of volunteers – small and light on their feet – to get out of here and steal us a handful of weapons. Bring them back and we can seize the ship and head for home. What the Spanish don't know is that right here in the gunroom is a little trap door leading to the bread room.' This I knew, for I had been in there once before. 'In the bread room, there's a door leading out to the after platform. And from there it's straight on to the gunners' storeroom, for which I have the key.' With a dramatic flourish Middlewych produced a brass key, about the size of a man's index finger.

'D'you think you might be able to nip down there and pick up a few weapons for us?' He said it in the breezy way my mother might have asked me to run down to the Rose and Crown and tell my father his dinner was ready.

'What about the guards?' I said.

'Yes, sir,' chimed in Richard. 'Isn't the ship crawling with sentries?'

'Yes,' said Middlewych. 'There's a Spanish marine on every companionway. I'm sure they're just itching for an excuse to run any one of us through with a bayonet. So, whatever you do, you must be very careful. But I think you'll find most of them seem to be carousing. One of our chaps got taken down there this evening to fix the pump and he says there are only two guards down in the hold. One by the after magazine and one by the forward magazine.'

I felt a familiar shudder of fear, and Richard and I exchanged wary glances.

'Is there anything else we need to know?' said Richard. He'd obviously made up his mind he was going already.

'Yes,' said Middlewych. 'The hold is flooded with six feet of water. Do either of you boys swim? Good!'

'How are we going to get past the sentries?' said Richard.

'It's going to be difficult,' admitted Middlewych. 'But here's a couple of ideas. First of all, Bouncer here has been hiding in my cabin since all this began. Take him with you and see if you can distract the after magazine sentry. Then you can swim your way forward, and see what's to be done when you get there. Whatever happens with these sentries, remember I don't want you killing either of them. If they find a dead sentry, they'll know something's up, and they may start bumping us all off.'

'Can I talk to Richard?' I asked the Lieutenant.

'Carry on, lad. Carry on.'

Ordinarily, I would not have dared talk to a senior officer in this way. But circumstances were very different. We were all prisoners now, and Middlewych was asking Richard and me to risk our lives.

We huddled together, away from the Lieutenant's earshot. 'He's asking a lot of us!' I said with some indignation.

Richard gave a weary shrug. 'The future's looking bleak enough already. The crew here are convinced we've got years ahead of us, rotting away in a Spanish prison. The way I see it, Sam, we've got a simple choice. We can attempt to escape tonight, and maybe die trying. Or we can waste away over the next few years dying of starvation or disease.'

Just at that moment I thought of Ben, stone dead with an axe in his head. I knew I had to do this.

'Let's give it a try.' Then we both grinned like the idiots we were.

'Death or glory!' said Richard.

'Death or glory!' said I.

It was so crowded in the gunroom that, with men standing and moving around, it was possible to ensure the guards outside could not see what we were doing. Within moments, we had set off. Down to the hold, on to the gunners' storeroom, back to the gunroom. On an ordinary day it was a job that would take three minutes . . . We squeezed through the narrow hatch and down into the bread locker. It was pitch black down there, so Middlewych passed down a lantern. Then he carefully lowered down Bouncer, and wished us luck.

'Take your time, boys. Getting back alive is the most important thing.'

Then the hatch shut over our heads, and Richard and I sat in the dim light of the lantern, waiting for our eyes to get used to the gloom. My heart was beating so hard I thought my chest was going to burst. I stroked Bouncer to stop him mewling, and breathed deeply to calm myself.

After a while, when we were ready, we began to pick our way through the provisions and towards the small door that led out to the after platform. This too was locked, and the key could only be inserted from the other side. To get past this barrier, Middlewych had given us a small screwdriver to take the lock from the door. Behind the door would be a sentry. Exactly where, we did not know. I tried to peek through a crack in the wood, but could see nothing. We listened very intently, but could hear nothing against the general hubbub of the fifty or so men above us. While I held the lantern up, Richard began, ever so gently, to remove the three screws that held the small lock in place. Every so often, one of the screws would creak as we turned it, or Richard's hand would slip, and the screwdriver would scrape against the wood.

We worked on that lock for an eternity and Richard and I were soon bathed in sweat. We had been given very little to drink by our captors, and I began to feel a powerful thirst. Eventually the lock came away from the door. Middlewych had warned us that the door creaked loudly when it was opened. We had a plan for this too. Richard went back to the hatch that led to the gunroom, and tapped gently upon it. Then he moved gingerly back to me by the door. We waited. After an interval, our men began to cheer and holler.

At that moment I pushed at the door. It did give an infernal creak – and I expected the Spanish guard to come tearing down the corridor and impale us both. But, thank heaven, with the noise from the gunroom, he never heard the door.

I opened it as far as it would go. There was just enough space for me to wriggle out. Richard followed immediately after with Bouncer, pulling the door closed behind him. Above the noise we could hear angry shouting from the guards upstairs. The noise in the gunroom simmered down as quickly as it had started.

On my hands and knees I crawled as quietly as I could down the small narrow corridor to the after platform. At every new plank I expected a squeak or creak to give me away. But the ship was so solidly constructed, nothing moved or made a noise.

Somewhere before me lay the sentry. I could smell him – the sweet odour of smouldering tobacco wafted down towards me – a welcome change from the usual stench of the hold. As I reached the corridor end I peered cautiously round the corner. There he was, sitting with his back to me, underneath the mess deck ladder. Yes, he was smoking a pipe – something any of us would be deservedly flogged for, so near to the magazine.

I glanced back at Richard, crouched by the breadroom door, and beckoned him to let go of Bouncer. I waved a morsel of pork – a leftover from the officers' last meal – and he trotted up to me curiously. Then I tossed the pork over to the far side of the after platform. Bouncer, wonderful Bouncer, followed on, padding up to the pork. Just before he pounced on it, he gave a delighted meow. The guard immediately sat up, and turned around to look. I peeked around the corner to see this great tall fellow, creeping cautiously towards the cat. Fortunately for us, he liked cats. 'Gato! Gato!' he was calling. Bouncer stayed exactly where he was, then playfully rolled over on to his back. At once, the guard rested his musket against the after platform rail, and crouched down to stroke the cat. Then he started speaking fondly to Bouncer. I had no idea what he was saying, but I quickly discovered what it was.

Underneath the after platform was a hatchway leading down to the fish room. The guard must have caught a whiff of fish as he stood there. He pulled the hatch up and peered down. 'Ah ha!' we heard him say, and he gingerly lowered himself down into the store. Richard and I needed no second bidding. We crept as quickly as silence would allow down the stairway to the hold, and into the dark murky flood water.

The water was not as cold as I'd expected it to be. If it had been freezing, I doubt whether Richard and I could have slipped gently into it without shivering in great convulsions. We were up to our necks when we heard the guard clamber out of the fish-room hatchway. Once out of our depth we cast off into the gloom, silent as swans towards the dim light at the far end of the ship. Here would be the next sentry, and only God knew how we would get past him.

The water was quite the most disgusting thing I have

ever lowered my body into, and I was relieved it was so dark in the hold that I could not really see what was both floating and swimming past me. I knew there were rats down there, and I did see some dark shapes scurry along the upper storage tiers, and drop into the water. But before it had flooded, the hold was also full of rubbish. Part of its notorious smell came from the turds lone sailors working down there would leave to avoid a trip to the heads in foul weather. Still, at least the scurrying and splashing of the rats might allow us some leeway with the guards when we made the occasional sound.

Moving so slowly, it took us several minutes to reach the bow of the *Miranda*. We spotted the other sentry propping up a rail on the forward platform long before we reached it. He was an amiable-looking fellow. Young but quite stout, and he too carried a musket with a bayonet. On the far side, not more than five feet away from where he stood, was the gunners' storeroom. Richard and I reached the stairway to the platform, and stopped. We looked at each other and raised our eyebrows as if to say, 'What the hell do we do now?'

Richard mouthed 'Wait?' and I nodded assent. Wait we did, until the water began to chill the very marrow of our bones. I started to shiver so much I began to worry that the ripples I was making were bound to give us away.

Then after what seemed like an eternity, a voice called down. 'Hola! Alejandro!' The man looked up. There followed a jovial and lively conversation. I guessed that his friends were tempting him to come up to the gun deck for a break and a drink. He shrugged and kept refusing. 'Go on! Go on!' I willed him. Richard kept nodding his head, and it was all I could do not to burst out laughing. He wouldn't go, although we could hear the reluctance in his voice. The other man muttered what I took to be a good-natured curse and left him.

Our sentry sighed forlornly, then he yawned and farted noisily, shaking a trouser leg as if to let the smell out. Then he lit his pipe. It wouldn't take. He cursed, and mind finally made up, he turned to climb the stairs. This was too good to be true. As soon as his legs disappeared through the hatch we edged up on to the platform. Just at that moment, an awful thought hit me. We would be leaving a trail of stinking water which would be quickly spotted as soon as the sentry returned.

I whispered to Richard, 'Lift me through the slats nearby the storeroom.' This he did. As I stood on the far side of the banister that separated the platform from the hold, I stripped off my shirt and trousers, leaving them in a soggy pile on a small ledge. I reached the storeroom door without having to walk over most of the forward platform. I quickly opened the storeroom, and collected a handful of cutlasses, knives and boarding axes. These I passed back to Richard, who was still in the water. Then I locked the door behind me, slipped back on my slimy clothes, and fitted as many weapons as I could carry around my belt. I wondered whether or not to carry a knife clenched between my teeth – as pirates were supposed to do. But the thought of swimming through that repulsive water without my mouth sealed tight put me off the idea.

Then we were gone. We were halfway back towards the stern before we heard the sentry returning. He settled down with some fresh tobacco, and I prayed he would not notice any tell-tale puddles.

Going back quietly was more difficult. Both of us were weighed down with as many heavy weapons as we could carry. When we eventually reached the after platform the same sentry was still there. We could do nothing but wait. At last, an officer came and called him upstairs. We emerged from the water and darted as quickly as we could to the safety of the bread-room hatch.

A great sensation of relief swept over me as we both huddled inside the dark storeroom. But as I leaned over to pull the door shut I saw at once that we had left a trail of dirty water in our wake. It was impossible to miss and led directly to the bread-room door. My stomach lurched at the thought of going out into the after platform again, but I knew it had to be done.

'Hang on a second,' I whispered to Richard, and wriggled out of the door again. I could see his face peeping out from the dark. He looked completely baffled.

A broom had been left in the corridor and I seized it at once to sweep over the water, leaving dank patches in the wood, rather than pools that had obviously just been made. As I finished I heard footsteps and conversation on the stair. I barely had time to close off the bread-room door and wedge it shut when the guard returned. Peeking through a crack in the door, I could see it was a different man. Even if he did notice the water, he would probably just assume it had been like that before he came down.

Then, with infinite caution, we crept through the dark bread room towards the tiny outline of light that shone around the gunroom hatch. I reached up and knocked gently. A brighter light flooded in as Lieutenant Middlewych's face appeared at the open hatch. Richard and I grinned like madmen and gave him a thumbs-up signal. Back in the gunroom, danger over, I began to feel the cold. I shivered so much I feared my friends would think I was trembling with fear. But we were quickly handed a couple of towels and a spare set of clothes. Middlewych himself gave me one of his shirts. After the rags I was used to wearing, it felt strange to put on such fine cotton clothing.

Stage one of our escape had gone to plan. Now all we had to do was seize the ship from our captors.

With Mandeville gone, Middlewych came into his own, and I could see a future captain in the making. First of all, he ensured a good number of men were standing around in front of us. Then we retired to the rear of the gunroom cabins, to the open space for the sweep of the tiller at the very stern of the ship. Here we could be sure of being out of sight of the guards.

'What have we got?' he asked himself aloud, carefully spreading the haul we had brought back from the storeroom. 'Three cutlasses, two boarding axes and seven swords. Well done, well done indeed! Now . . . a cutlass for me, who else'll take one?'

Rather to my surprise, Silas volunteered at once. I caught his eye, and he winked. 'It's a job that's got to be done, lad,' he said.

Robert Neville, who had been listening closely, stepped forward too. Middlewych was courteous and diplomatic.

'Mr Neville, this is indeed a brave offer – but I need a real bruiser to take this weapon.' We could see his point. Robert was still a lad, like us. Anyone carrying one of our precious cutlasses had to be able to use it to maximum effect. I wondered how Robert must have felt having to hand over his splendid new dirk to his captors.

'You will have a role in this enterprise, though,' Middlewych said to Neville. 'As soon as we overpower the guards outside the door, you will lead a party to scour the ship for other weapons. The sooner we arm our lads here, the sooner we can seize the ship.'

Then Middlewych had word discreetly passed around the gunroom asking for men who were skilled at throwing knives and axes. He was spoiled for choice.

There were too many of us crowded into the gunroom, so a good few men were sitting just outside its open door, in the rear of the mess. They would have to remain as ignorant of our activity as the guards. A few yards further on from them, in a half circle, were a squad of ten Spanish marines sat on stools and barrels, keeping a bored eye on us. The bayonets on their muskets glimmered in the dim light of the lanterns, but they were drooping – much like the men's eyelids. No doubt the Spaniards were resentful that they had had to watch us while the rest of their comrades celebrated.

Middlewych whispered a few more orders, and then we waited. 'When the noise upstairs dies down,' he said, 'that'll be when they've drunk their fill. Then we'll wait another half hour for them to get to sleep. That'll be when the guards are at their lowest ebb, and that'll be when we'll strike. Until then, let's just have a little nap and wait. Put the word round. All of us to settle down and appear to be asleep.'

Nap? I was too anxious to nap. I hated this waiting before we fought. I longed to spring into action and get this bloody business over with. I leaned over the door to look at the guards. There they were, unaware of what we had in store. What were they thinking about, as they sat there, dull eyes peering at us through the gloom?

Bouncer came over to me, and curled up in my lap. He still had a faint whiff of the fish he had been given earlier. Now he wanted a warm place to rest and a kind hand to stroke him to sleep. As the cat purred, the whole weight of the day rolled over me like a gigantic wave. Despite my fear I felt exhausted. I lapsed into semi-sleep, although my thoughts drifted again and again to the face of the man I had killed.

Richard shook me roughly awake, and Bouncer trotted off with an irritated meow, tail in the air. 'Are you coming with me and Neville?' he said.

I nodded. If this was going to work, we all had to act together as quickly as possible.

The ship had now settled into a still silence. Not for long. As quietly as we could we stirred any sleeping comrades and prepared to leap into action.

Beyond the open door were the ten marines. Not all of them appeared to be awake. Gingerly Middlewych distributed the daggers and axes, and gave each man a target. Nine men, four one side of the open gunroom door, five the other. There were not enough weapons to tackle each Spaniard but, with luck, we would not need them all.

If they had rehearsed their moves, Middlewych's assassins could not have done a better job. On his signal they moved stealthily out of the door, throwing knives or axes into the guards. Only the first four were needed. As each guard started and fell to the floor, our own men near to him rose from the deck and dragged him down. Other guards, who were half asleep, were quietly overpowered. The sailors at the door stopped throwing their weapons for fear of hitting their own. The guards were quickly dragged into the gunroom. A couple were dead, and two others were badly wounded and had to be tightly gagged to stop them crying out. The rest of them had simply been seized and were all too eager to surrender.

The whole exercise had been carried through with barely a sound. We listened for any sign that our rebellion had been overheard, but none was evident.

'Let's see what's happening on deck,' said Middlewych.

Our cache of weapons was growing by the minute. Ten muskets and bayonets, and several more knives and pistols carried by the guards, were swiftly distributed. Robert, with admirable aplomb, pulled a knife from the body of one of the dead guards.

Then he, Richard and I crept over to the ladder leading directly to the storeroom. We peered down. A guard was still there, but he had propped his musket against the hatch rail and was sitting on his haunches, smoking his pipe. We did not even have to kill him. Quick as a flash Robert leaped down the ladder, snatched his musket and pointed the bayonet at his stomach. The man stared, mouth wide open, too shocked to speak. Robert put his finger to his mouth and whispered a stern 'Shhhh', and Richard and I hurried to the storeroom. Sweating copiously, and with our hearts in our mouths, we hurriedly gathered another armful of cutlasses and daggers. Then we went back up to the mess deck. It was still quiet. Middlewych and the rest of the men were poised ready to take this endeavour to its final stage.

Robert turned to Richard. 'Buckley, take this fellow back to the gunroom and have him wait with the rest of his friends. I'm sure the Lieutenant has arranged a guard, so perhaps you'll join us upstairs?'

I was struck by Robert's manner. I could scarcely believe he was the same fearful boy I had seen crying on the orlop deck a few weeks previously.

We returned to the mess-deck ladder. Middlewych nodded abruptly, and beckoned me over.

'Witchall – nip up there and see what's going on,' he whispered.

I crept up one step at a time and peered through the rail. All around the gun deck were the huddled, sleeping forms of Spanish sailors – the men who had been left to repair the *Miranda* and sail us back to port. There was a guard there too, with his back to the hatchway, over-looking his comrades.

Middlewych ordered one of our marines to seize the sentry, then he turned again to us. 'Let's pay a visit to the Captain's cabin. Buckley, Warandel, Witchall, come with me. Neville, when we've dealt with the guard, set the rest of our men up to surround this lot on the gun deck. Unless there's any trouble, wait for my orders. Let's try to do this with as little bloodshed as possible.'

Our marine glided up the stairs, dagger in hand, and silently despatched the unwary guard. As our men crept among the Spanish crew, the four of us tiptoed on to the cabin. The door, already half ajar, creaked as Middlewych opened it further. A sleepy voice called out in Spanish, and Silas immediately leaped over to the source of the sound. In the dim moonlight, I could see a young man in officer's uniform stretched out on Mandeville's cot, which he had placed on the floor. Before he could say any more, Silas had a knife at his throat, and Middlewych was talking to him in Spanish.

'Yes, yes,' the officer replied, speaking to us at once in English. 'Very well, sir. The ship is yours. I will tell my men to surrender.'

'Make sure you do,' said Middlewych coldly. 'My man here is all too eager to slit your throat.'

And that was it. The Spanish officer, closely guarded by three of our men, went over to his crew and ordered them to stir themselves. Surrounded as they were, he could see they were outnumbered, and there seemed little point in trying to resist us. There were only thirty or so of them. They had been foolish to leave so few to repair the ship and guard us. Perhaps they thought that after our defeat the fight had gone out of us. His men stirred in the dim lantern light, and we swiftly herded them down to the gunroom. Meanwhile, Middlewych took the Spanish officer on a quick tour, to round up any sentries scattered around the ship.

I felt utterly spent. All around me my comrades were laughing and bellowing like mad men – as if they could not believe their good fortune. I wandered through the wreckage of the ship, still only partially repaired, and went to find a quiet spot on the orlop deck. Here I sat down and cried. I felt so happy to have survived this ordeal, but weighed down with the terror I had felt and the horror I had lived through. Soon after, Tom Shepherd came to sit with me and place a consoling arm around my shoulder. Then, to my surprise, he recited a poem.

'What is the price of experience? Do men buy it for
a song?
Or wisdom for a dance in the street? No, it is
bought with the price
Of all a man hath, his house, his wife, his children.
Wisdom is sold in the desolate market where none
come to buy,
And in the wither'd field where the farmer plows
for bread in vain . . .'

'My friend William, from London, he told me that. I
can't remember any more.'

I made Tom write it down for me.

Tom continued to talk softly to me. 'And if you have
to fight again, you'll know what to expect, and you'll be
much better prepared for it. And you'll know how to
survive. But going through all this . . . you have to pay
for it, don't you?'

Now all we had to do was sail an undermanned, badly
damaged frigate back home through winter storms and
several hundreds of miles of enemy seas.

CHAPTER 13

The Home Shore

The dawn was a fine one – a calm sea, and the promise of a sunny day. We all knew we had no time to waste repairing the ship, and making good our escape. During the course of the day Middlewych was everywhere – encouraging, cajoling, hounding and praising. By eight bells that afternoon we had rigged up a jury foremast. With that, and our tattered mizzenmast, we set all sails to return home to England.

In the evening Middlewych gave orders for the cook to prepare the best feast he could muster. But it was a sorry affair. Much of our food had been ruined by the rising waters in the hold. In fact, it was lucky there were so few of us left to feed, otherwise we may have had to make a dangerous return to Gibraltar to reprovision. There was to be no extra grog either – we would not be making the same mistake as our Spanish friends, and celebrating too much too soon. The thirty or so prisoners we took when we regained our ship were kept confined to the Captain's cabin. The guards who stood watching them at the open doors were changed every hour. There on the gun deck we also took the precaution of setting up a carronade filled with grapeshot. This was constantly manned and pointed straight at an open door to the Captain's cabin.

Despite our repairs, the *Miranda* was a shadow of her former self – especially with our mainmast still missing. The timbers at the side of the ship had been particularly badly damaged. Now there was a constant need for men to man the pumps to keep the water in the hold from rising further. Here we made use of our prisoners in this task – letting them out two at a time from the Captain's cabin. Middlewych ensured their cooperation by telling them that if they didn't work they would not eat. Most of the Spaniards seemed to be grateful to still be alive. Like us, most had been compelled to serve on their ships. As long as they behaved, we bore them no ill will.

The wind blew in our favour, and we made good

speed. Within days, as the *Miranda* sailed north, we could feel the weather getting cooler. But that return journey was a melancholy one. With so many dead or taken prisoner, the mess seemed three-quarters empty. Still, it had its compensations. Officers and midshipmen mingled more freely with the ratings, and I learned a little more about Robert Neville. The voyage had been the making of him, and it was difficult now to imagine he had ever been the snivelling boy I had once watched being reprimanded by his uncle. Lieutenant Spencer had survived the battle, but had been one of those taken off on the *Gerona*. Robert fretted about him to me. He was fond of his uncle, despite the Lieutenant's harsh words. I learned too that Robert's family were wealthy, influential people. His father, Viscount Neville, held a senior position at the Admiralty.

When time allowed, Robert taught me some of his seafaring skills. I learned how to use a sextant to calculate the ship's position on a map, and how the constellations could be used to establish our direction. Robert was full of fascinating information, which he was keen to share. In me he found a willing pupil. Although my father had encouraged me to take an interest in the world, and develop what he termed 'a well-furnished mind', he had a blind spot when it came to science. Especially any scientific discovery which conflicted with his religious beliefs.

Robert's father, in contrast, was especially interested in the new science of geology. He loved to poke around in the ground, studying fossils and the varying layers of soil and rock beneath the surface of the land. Most of all, said Robert, he loved to debate the nature of the formation of the Earth. Before he went to sea, Robert had sat at the family dining table listening to his father's friends and relations discuss these very topics, and what he had to say filled me with curiosity. Why was it, they would argue, that the remains of ancient sea creatures could be found on top of high mountains such as those of the Alps?

'I could tell you that,' I said. 'They were swept up there during the great flood, when God covered the Earth with water.'

'Yes,' said Robert. 'That's what my Uncle Henry says. But then, he would. He's Bishop of Chichester. You and him, you're what we call Neptunists.' I was flattered to be placed alongside a bishop. Then Robert went on, 'Uncle Henry believes the world was created exactly as it is – mountains, hills, rivers and valleys – all in the first week of creation.'

'So do I,' I chimed in. 'Let the waters under the heaven be gathered together unto one place, and let the dry land appear: and it was so. On the third day of creation, in fact. It's all there in the first book of Genesis.'

'Yes, yes,' said Robert impatiently. 'And they say if

anything has changed then it's due to the action of the seas during times of great flooding. But there's another school of thought here. My father and I, we're Plutonists.

'We think that volcanoes and earthquakes, and the wind and the rain and the sea, all change the face of the planet. We think that the mountains with the fossils of sea creatures at the top used to be part of the sea bed, and they've risen up. All of this, though, has taken place over an extremely long period of time. Hundreds of thousands, or perhaps millions, of years . . .'

I couldn't agree with him. 'But Reverend Chatham told us the world was created in 4004BC, on Sunday 23rd October. So it's less than six thousand years old. So that puts paid to your explanation.'

'That's another argument altogether,' said Robert. He was beginning to sound impatient. 'That's the case if you want to take the Bible literally. My father would argue that the Book of Genesis is an allegory.'

'A what?' said I.

'It's not meant to be taken literally. I believe in the same God as you, Witchall, but I think some parts of the Bible are open to interpretation.' Robert was getting impatient, and determined to have the final word. '"There are more things in heaven and earth, Horatio, than are dreamt of in your philosophy."'

I felt quite baffled.

'It's *Hamlet*, Witchall. Y' know, Shakespeare? He's the fellow who came up with the name of our ship.'

I didn't. Shakespeare was another world too. Robert was losing me fast. He did annoy me when he made me feel stupid.

Luck was with us throughout that journey. The wind blew fair, and no pirates, privateers or enemy frigates crossed our path. We would have been the easiest prize in the Atlantic Ocean. Eventually, on the morning of 14th February 1801, Lizard Point, on the southern tip of Cornwall, came into view. Our home shore, and Valentine's Day too! This seemed like a good omen. As we crowded on to the larboard side of the deck to peer through the haze at the far-off coast, I could see the delight and relief on everyone's faces.

Our home port of Portsmouth was only a couple of days' sailing away, but Middlewych decided it would be safer to head for Plymouth, which was much nearer. Perhaps now we only had one more day at sea. I finally allowed myself to believe that I would soon be seeing my family and Rosie again. I'd never felt happier.

It didn't last. When I mentioned this to Robert, he gave me a wry smile. 'I don't think the Navy will let you go, Sam.'

I knew he was going to say something that would crush my spirit. He usually called me Witchall, as I called him Mr Neville. I thought of him as 'Robert' and it seemed odd for me to have to address a boy no more than a year or two older than me in this formal way, but such were the traditions of the Royal Navy.

Robert continued: 'If you're pressed, you have to remain on your ship until it pays off, or you're turned over to another ship. They may let you go when the war is over – although heaven knows when that may be.'

'But don't I get shore leave?' I said, feeling my face grow hot with anger.

'I'm amazed that you never discussed this with your messmates,' he replied.

'I never thought to ask about it.'

Robert sighed. 'Men aren't usually allowed to leave their ship, never mind go home and be expected to come back. The Navy is afraid they'll just disappear. As soon as we get back to Portsmouth we'll all be transferred to other Navy ships while the *Miranda* is given a refit.'

I felt a numb disappointment for the rest of the morning. The elements, too, conspired to match my mood. The sky darkened and rain began to fall in sheets. Soon after we passed Lizard Point, it became obvious that we were heading into the teeth of a storm.

When the wind picked up, sails were ripped from the yards as we struggled to furl them. With only sixty of us left, and all weary from the voyage, the ship seemed too big for us to handle. Left completely at the mercy of wind and tide, the *Miranda* began to drift perilously close to the rocky shore.

All of the crew had more to do than any one man could be expected to achieve. We raced from side to side, drenched by the storm and exhausted by our failing efforts. The *Miranda*'s four heavy anchors were dropped in a bid to halt our fatal drift. The rolling and pitching of the ship put an enormous strain on the anchor cables. As late afternoon faded to dusk these cables groaned as if under torture. Soon after dark there was an horrendous splintering of wood and cable as first one anchor, and then the others, parted company with the ship.

In a final frantic effort to regain control of our ship, Middlewych ordered the guns and stores thrown into the sea. The task of casting loose these two-ton guns, and letting them smash through the side of the ship as it heaved to and fro, was exhausting and dangerous, and two men were crushed. Theirs was a gruesome death, and Dr Claybourne had only brandy to ease their final moments.

Lighter stores followed the guns. The ship's spare sails, spars, ropes – anything we could bring up from the rapidly flooding hold – were hurled overboard.

During the night, in howling wind and sheets of rain, the ship shuddered and lurched, throwing us all to the deck. We had been driven aground a hundred yards from the shore. Soon after, the rudder tore off with a sickening splinter. Yardarms crashed to the deck, then our recently repaired foremast toppled into the sea. I was grateful it had lasted that long. Just as scurvy attacks the body's frail points, opening up old wounds healed long before, so the sea did its worst to our ship. The *Miranda* began to break up, as tons of water tormented her weakened hull. Carpenters' repairs burst open against the pressure of the waves. Water cascaded into the interior, and the ship's pumps could no longer hold the rising torrent. Soon the hold was submerged, and stinking black water oozed, sloshed, then poured up the stairwells to the mess deck, filling it to a waterline that rose and fell with the tide. At dusk on 15th February, Middlewych called for all hands to abandon ship.

Before we made our preparations to leave, Robert and I accompanied the Lieutenant to the Captain's quarters. When the storm had begun, all hands had been called to help save the ship. The prisoners had been locked into the cabin, with no men spare to guard them. Middlewych turned the key in the lock, expecting the prisoners to rush forward to escape. But instead, we found them sitting defeated on the floor – all seasick and pale with fear. Middlewych spoke quickly with their commanding officer. The two men shook hands, and the Spanish officer turned to address his men.

As he spoke, Middlewych turned to Robert. 'I've told him they're to try to reach the shore as best they can, then surrender themselves to the authorities. He's given me his word as a gentleman that he will order his men to give themselves up. I can't see any other way around it. The alternative is to kill them, and I don't have the heart to do that.'

Soon after, a group of us tried to lower the longboat into the boiling sea. The ship's other boats had been lost in the storm or crushed by falling yards. Middlewych had given orders that men who could not swim were to have priority on the boat. But before anyone could clamber aboard it was swept away by a huge wave, and overturned. There was nothing else to do now but to take our chances in the water.

During these last few hours I had often thought of Ben. What would he be doing? What advice or comfort would he have to offer? Now anarchy reigned. Discipline had collapsed.

I told Richard what I had seen. 'I suppose the men've given up hope of getting home alive,' he said. 'They're determined to die happy. Either that, or they're trying to give themselves enough Dutch courage to take to the water.'

In those final minutes aboard, a thought hit me like a thunderbolt. If I could get away from the ship, then I could get away from the Navy! If I survived, then I would be free from this floating prison. There would be nothing to stop me from heading for home. I pushed the notion to the back of my mind. For now, there were too many 'ifs' to consider . . .

As the ship emptied, we grabbed whatever objects we thought would help us make our way to the shore. I found myself on the quarterdeck with Silas and Richard. They looked as desperate as I felt. We were all numb from the cold, and worn out by our struggle to save the ship.

Standing over a fallen yardarm, I shouted at Richard over the noise of the storm, 'Help me cut a piece off this!' He nodded, and as we began to hack away with boarding axes, Silas joined us.

'I'm going to get home, and so are you two,' he told us with some determination. 'We've not been through all this just to die in sight of a friendly shore. Now let's lash some rope to this yard, so we've got something to hang on to.'

Over the chaos of the storm I heard a plaintive whine. It was Bouncer – so drenched and bedraggled his fur hung tight and soaking round his body.

'What are we going to do with the cat?' I shouted.

Silas had an idea. 'Put him in a chest and set him off to the shore. He'll drown if any of us try to carry him.' So that we did – there were plenty of wooden chests to choose from, and I chose Ben's. Inside were his spare set of clothes and some meagre possessions. It brought a lump to my throat. Here were a few letters from his wife, Caitlin. Neither of them could read or write, so they kept in touch with letters written and read by friends. Ben never let me read or write his letters. This was a part of his life he wanted to keep to himself. Also there in the chest was a silhouette portrait of Caitlin which Ben had treasured, and a model ship he was making for his son. That was all he left to the world. I'd hoped to find his wife's double-heart brooch, which he carried as a good luck charm. But that was probably lying with him at the bottom of the sea.

I flattened down the clothes, dropped Bouncer in, then put the letters, silhouette and boat back in too. If the chest did reach the shore, maybe someone would return these possessions to Ben's family?

We lowered the chest into the sea and watched the waves carry it away.

'Let's be away ourselves,' said Silas. By now the *Miranda* was listing badly, and the larboard side of the quarterdeck was almost level with the sea. All three of us dragged over our piece of yardarm, and prepared to launch ourselves into the chilly water. Then, among the few frantic souls still aboard the ship, I noticed Robert Neville, standing as best he could on the sloping quarterdeck.

'Mr Neville, are you not leaving the ship?' I yelled in astonishment.

'Never was a great one for the water, Witchall,' he replied. Then his composure cracked a little. 'Sam, I can't swim. I'm going to stay here until the storm abates, and take my chances then.'

Silas joined us. 'Bollocks to that,' he said. 'This ship is breaking up. You're coming with us.' With that, he frog-marched the young midshipman down the sloping deck and over to the side of the ship.

And so all four of us slid into the sea and began kicking our legs in the water for all we were worth. I expected it to be extremely chilly, but we were so cold already, it made little difference to us. The last thing I saw on deck was Lieutenant Middlewych trying to persuade some drunken sailors to take their chances in the water. My heart went out to him. He was doing his duty to the end, and I was sure he would not leave the ship until the last man had gone. I hoped in my heart we would see him again, safe on land.

Through driving rain, the silhouette of the rocky shore bobbed in and out of view. Our clothes weighed heavy on our weary limbs, and each exertion required considerable effort. Robert was close to panic. His grip kept slipping from the rope wrapped around the yard. Richard and I did our best to grab hold of him and return him, coughing and spluttering, to the surface.

As we drifted in the waves, hurled high and low in

great troughs of water, a strong current picked us up and carried us along the coast. Silas shouted, 'Just hold on for dear life, lads. Maybe this will carry us to a more friendly-looking shore?'

Then a huge wave crashed down upon us, and I was snatched away from the yardarm and swept beneath the water . . . As I sank deeper my ears began to ache and I was gripped by a fierce terror. The wave had caught me so completely by surprise, I had not even filled my lungs before I went under. Now my chest was aching desperately for air. Almost by instinct, I found myself gulping down great lungfuls of water. So was this what it was like to drown? I flailed beneath the sea, trying to move my legs and arms hard enough to propel me to the surface. But in those dark waters I did not even know which way was up and which was down.

The strength was fast leaving my limbs. Panic subsided and a strange stillness overtook me. I surrendered myself to death and felt at peace with the world. In my mind's eye I saw myself as a young child, snug with my brother between my mother and father, safe and sound in my parents' bed.

Then, an undercurrent thrust me unexpectedly to the surface, and there I was again, back in the world of the living – spluttering for air and coughing up huge salty globs of mucus and sea water. Ahead of me was a broken rail from the *Miranda*'s quarterdeck, and I grabbed at it, clinging on for dear life. My head spun as I felt sick and dizzy. Maybe twenty yards in front of me, I could glimpse Silas and the two boys still clinging on to their yardarm. Richard was shouting, almost in a frenzy, and looking around desperately. His shrieks carried across the waves. 'SAAAMM!!!! SAAAAMMM!!!' When I reached the crest of a wave I shouted and shouted, and waved one hand until they spotted me. I kicked my legs hard in the water until I managed to rejoin them.

By now we had been in the water perhaps twenty minutes, and I was so cold I could barely manage to maintain my grip on the wooden rail. But the shore was looming out of the darkness, and salvation was at hand.

'Come on, you bastards!' said Silas. 'We're nearly there.'

Spluttering through the spray, we gained strength as the shore grew closer. Then, all of a sudden, I felt rough pebbles beneath my feet. It was my first touch of solid ground in six months.

'We're almost there!' I shouted. Then a large wave crashed into my back and threw me face down into the water. I struggled to my feet and broke surface, gasping for air. Just at that moment the backwash caught me and carried me out to sea. As I was thrown back I caught a glimpse of the dark outlines of the other three, now only waist deep in the water and wading towards the beach. Again, panic seized me. *Don't let me die now, please, God. Not when I'm so near to the shore.*

Before I was swept under I cried out, and one of the silhouettes turned and began to swim back towards me. 'Hold on, Sam! Hold on!' a voice called urgently. It was Richard. As he half-swam, half-waded out to me, another wave picked me up and thrust me nearer to the shore. Now I was so weak I could barely force my frozen limbs to fight against the motion of the tide. Richard grabbed my arm and held me firm as the outgoing water tried to tug me back into the dark sea and certain death.

We staggered out of the water, plodding through the surf, wet clothes dragging us down, and on to the soft wet sand of the beach. We lay there panting for five minutes or more, like gasping fish flailing on the deck of a fishing vessel. But, far from writhing in our death throes, we rolled around in triumph.

'We did it!' we shrieked, scarcely believing we had reached dry land.

Up from the beach we could see the lights of a village. We stumbled up the cliff path to the church and banged on the door of the vicarage. A small man wearing spectacles opened the door. He stared in mute astonishment at the four bedraggled figures standing before him. Robert Neville reasserted his authority.

'Good evening, sir,' he said with ridiculous formality for a boy who looked like a drowned rat. 'I am the Honourable Robert Neville, and these are my shipmates from His Majesty's ship *Miranda* – shipwrecked just now close to Lizard Point. Would you be so kind as to take us in and provide a little warmth and a change of clothing?'

The parson raised his eyebrows. 'This is the village of Pentherick, young sir. It is in fact some thirty miles further east of Lizard Point.' We were all astounded by how much further the storm had swept us up the coast.

Our parson was a helpful fellow – or rather, he knew just the people who would help us. I stared past his shoulder with some longing at the blazing fire inside his house, but rather than ask us in he took us at once to the local inn. It was called the Royal Oak. The landlord, he explained on the way, was an old sea salt, who would be pleased to provide for us. Sure enough, our clothes were taken off to dry, and fresh ones provided. They were ill-fitting, but who could possibly grumble? The landlord told us he would gladly provide food, lodging and ale, but would most certainly prevail upon us to tell our extraordinary tale. It seemed a fair exchange.

CHAPTER 14

Uncertain Future

Later that evening, when the crowd of excited listeners had drifted away to their homes or other corners and rooms, we sat around the tavern fire. The landlord brought Silas, Robert, Richard and me thick roast beef sandwiches covered with horseradish sauce, and tankards of ale. In that moment I felt a rush of pure joy. I had gone away to sea, faced terrible perils, and survived. Here I was now, with fine food and drink, surrounded by my friends.

Silas turned and spoke directly to me. 'What now, Sam? You could just vanish into the night with me, and never set foot on a Navy ship again. The storm's blown itself out now, so let's make hay . . . the Navy wouldn't come looking for us – they'd assume we were drowned.'

Robert looked embarrassed, and took a great interest in the darkened view out of the window. We all knew he would not be reporting this conversation to anyone – he owed us all too much.

I pictured the scene in my head. News of the shipwreck would reach my parents. My mother would be consumed with grief. My father would burn with anger. Then – what an entrance – a few days later I would return up the garden path, rattle the knocker, and they would think they were seeing a ghost. It would be a blissful moment!

I looked at Richard and Robert. They would certainly be returning to the nearest Royal Dockyard, which would be Plymouth, a day or so's coachride from here.

Silas broke into my chain of thought. 'Well, Sam? Are you coming?'

'I don't know, Silas. Don't think I haven't considered it . . .' I replied. 'But I need to sleep on it.'

Silas was determined to make the best of his opportunity. This was as good a time as any. He had dry clothes, and a full belly. 'Word will have reached Plymouth that the *Miranda*'s been wrecked. The telegraph stations will convey the news to Portsmouth and the Admiralty by the end of the day . . . I'll be off before any pressmen or marines come snooping. I bid you all farewell.'

Robert chipped in, wary but resigned. 'I shall report you swept away to sea during the shipwreck. Mind that you change your name though, Mr Warandel. I wish you good luck.'

As Silas rose from his seat I rushed forward to hug him. I felt a great rush of affection for this weather-beaten sea dog. We were all survivors and now he was going to take back the life he'd had snatched away from him.

'You're a good lad, Sam,' he said as he hugged me back, then he was gone.

After Silas left, Richard went to the bar to fetch the three of us another round of ale. The drink was much stronger than the watered-down beer we were given on the *Miranda*. I began to feel quite woozy, and stared into the fire. While Richard and Robert talked, I thought of my family and Rosie, and wondered when I would ever see them again.

A sharp rapping made me look away from the fire, and up to the tavern window. Maybe Bouncer was out there – unaccustomed to solid earth and vegetation – making his way towards lights, human conversation and the smell of roasting meat. Perhaps, any minute, he would leap up to the sill, and begin scratching at the window.

*   *   *

The next morning I rose early. The sensation of being alone in a room was foreign to me. Although I had slept solidly, it was an odd feeling to be in a bed that did not roll with the swell of the sea. Downstairs I found Richard and Robert sitting around a table in the bar, eating eggs and bacon.

A plate arrived for me, along with a mug of tea. A piping hot egg with a runny yolk. Crispy rind on salty bacon. A slice of fresh bread with fresh butter. After months of rancid butter on hard biscuit, lukewarm slop and brackish water, it tasted so marvellous that I doubted that King George himself were eating a better breakfast.

Robert spoke first. 'We didn't really expect to see you this morning.'

Then Richard. 'So, Sam, are you heading for the hills? Is it the outlaw life for you?'

He made it sound like a great adventure.

Robert said, 'You could still get away, if you go this morning. But news of a shipwreck travels quickly. Wait until this afternoon, and you're asking for trouble.'

I was touched that he was urging me to go. I was still undecided.

Then Richard spoke up. 'After breakfast, let's walk down to the coast, and see if we can spot what's left of the *Miranda*. Come on, Sam. Come and bid a final farewell to your ship.'

The idea appealed to me. 'Yes, I'll do that. And maybe we can look for Ben's sea chest along the shoreline?'

Our generous landlord provided us with three warm coats, and we ventured out into a stark February morning. We wandered a half mile along the coastal path before the *Miranda* came into view. From where we stood on a cliff top, which sloped down to a drab pebble beach, we could see the pitiful state the ship was in. The masts and bowsprit were gone, and the wreck of the ship lay floundering in the low tide, with only the bow still well clear of the water.

Robert put a hand around my shoulder and spoke. 'Sam, you and Mr Warandel were right to drag me away. I shall always be grateful to you . . .'

I felt embarrassed by this unaccustomed show of affection. I could not think of anything appropriate to say.

'Well, Mr Neville – I'm sure we'd have attempted to rescue anyone we saw on the deck.'

'Even Lewis Tuck?' said Richard.

We all laughed.

'No, not him. Do either of you know whether he survived the battle?' I asked.

Richard spoke up. 'I saw him impaled with a boarding pike, just as the Spanish swept on to our deck. He was right there on the rail – balanced on the edge of the ship. As he fell into the sea, a shark popped its head out of the water and made off with him tight between its jaws.'

I was astounded. What a fate!

'No?' I gasped.

'No, Sam. I'm afraid not. Tuck was taken off to the *Gerona*.'

I didn't know whether to be pleased or disappointed.

We walked on. Soon we came to a stretch of beach where debris from the shipwreck had been brought in by the tide. Here was the tangled mess of the mizzen-mast, there was the bowsprit. Bits and pieces of the ship lay scattered all around. A few bodies too lay bobbing in the surf at the water's edge.

We made our way down the cliff and wandered among the wreckage. Amid this destruction, I began to feel guilty wishing my enemy Lewis Tuck dead. Whenever we came to a body we would drag it out of the water by the arms and turn it over away from the water line. We recognised them all of course, apart from a couple of the Spanish prisoners, but none were men I knew well.

'No sign of Ben's chest here, Sam,' said Richard. 'D'you want to look over at the next cove? There's bound to be some more debris there.'

I wasn't so sure. I did not want to waste precious time in Pentherick if I was going to vanish into the country-side and hope the naval authorities took me for dead. I hesitated.

'Let's get back, then,' said Richard. 'Come on, Sam. If you're going, you better go soon before a squad of marines turns up in the village looking for those Spanish sailors.'

I thought of Bouncer, trapped in that tea chest, his pathetic mewing lost in the wind of an empty beach. The tide was out sufficiently far for it to be possible to reach the next cove without returning up the cliffs.

'I'll just have a look over here,' I shouted, and ran quickly round the jagged rocks at the edge of the shoreline and on to the next beach.

It was a forlorn place, a great expanse of grey sand, grey sea and grey sky, deserted save for a few remnants washed ashore from the ship, and a scattering of bodies on the shoreline. I hurriedly began to search among the objects on the beach. But several I thought that might be boxes turned out to be rocks.

After a while, Richard appeared at the edge of the cove, and attracted my attention by whistling. His voice drifted across the empty beach, half-drowned by the crashing of the waves.

'Here, come on, Sam. We're going back to the Royal Oak.'

I waved and yelled, 'I'll catch you up.'

Fighting back my fear that I was running out of time, I began to search more desperately. Perhaps I should try further up the coast? But then the low sun poked out from the clouds and a watery light spread over the sand. At that moment my eye alighted on a sharp, dark shape in the middle distance that I had hitherto thought to be a rock. In the sunlight I could see its texture more clearly. It was a small wooden chest. I ran closer. It had been tipped on one edge and was half buried in the wet sand. There on its side in fading black ink were the words 'Benjamin Lovett'. I pulled it out and placed it upright. An agitated mewl came from within. I flipped back the latch and there was Bouncer, shivering in three or four inches of water, drenched and miserable, but still alive. He sprang out, ran three or four times round in a circle, shook his fur, then padded back to me. He looked up with what I took to be some indignation. 'Meoowwww?' he complained. I picked him up and nestled him inside my coat.

Inside the chest, Ben's letters and the silhouette of his wife were a soggy, waterlogged mess. But his model boat was still intact. I picked it up and ran back to the neighbouring beach.

'Hey! Come and look at this!' I shouted to Richard and Robert – now receding figures in the distance. My voice carried in the wind, and they stopped and turned round.

I ran towards them, gripping Bouncer tightly in my coat. When I reached my friends he poked his head out of my coat and gave another meow. Robert grinned.

'Well done, Sam. Perseverance wins the day.'

Then I held up Ben's boat. 'This was for his son,' I said.

Robert took it from me. 'Let me pay to have it delivered to him,' he said firmly. 'Perhaps you could write a letter for the lad and Mr Lovett's wife, to go with the parcel?'

Before we turned back from the beach I took a long final look at the wreck of the *Miranda*. I thought especially of my Sea Daddy Ben, lying on the ocean floor five miles off the coast of Spain. I couldn't bear to think of him at the bottom of the sea, his bones picked clean by scavenging sea creatures. Instead I tried to picture him there with a tankard of fine ale, a garland of seaweed and a brace of bonny mermaids for company.

By now it was mid-morning. I had still not decided what to do. Should I stay or should I go?

'We're heading for Plymouth,' said Robert. 'From there, they'll probably send us back to Portsmouth and a new ship.'

If I was going to escape, I had to go now. The prospect of returning to the comforts of my home and family, wooing Rosie, and escaping from the tyranny of the Navy all filled my imagination like a wondrous vision. But even if I did get away, what then? First of all, I had to get myself home. I was wearing clothes kindly lent to me by the Royal Oak landlord, and I couldn't bring myself to steal them. And I had a rich brown skin that marked me out at once as a sailor away from the sea. That would fade soon enough, but then what? I would live the rest of my life as a fugitive and an impostor. If I returned home, news would surely get back to the authorities. But it was not just the threat of capture and a certain flogging that held me back. The loss of my ship grieved me and I knew now that the sea was in my bones. Aboard the *Miranda*, I had found friends and comrades for whom I felt a fierce loyalty. Two of them were with me now.

Richard put his hand on my shoulder. 'What's it to be, Sam?'

'I'm staying with you,' I said quietly.

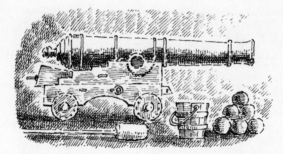

Acknowledgements

I'm especially grateful to my agent Charlie Viney who inspired this book by encouraging me to have a go at writing fiction. Children's books consultant Alison Stanley gave me useful help during the book's early stages, and Dilys Dowswell offered invaluable advice on all my first drafts.

At Bloomsbury Ele Fountain patiently helped shape the narrative and hone the style while Georgia Murray ensured the nuts and bolts of the story were tightened securely. Maritime expert Nicholas Blake gave generous advice on the historic and technical aspects of the book. I was not able to make all his recommended changes, for which I apologise both to him and anyone else more steeped than me in the salty subject of Nelson's Navy. Phillip Beresford and Katherine Grimes were responsible for the elegant look of the book, and Ian Butterworth created the evocative cover. Peter Bailey's fine line drawings decorate the inside pages.

Thank you to Kate Lee, Caroline Yates and Leslie Harris for their loan of valuable reference material, and also the staff of the National Maritime Museum Library, Greenwich, and Wolverhampton and Birmingham Public and Reference Libraries for their help during the researching of this book. A bibliography detailing some of the sources used can be found on pp 281–4.

I would also like to thank Anna Claybourne, Alex Costello, Fergus Fleming, Lucy Lethbridge, William and Debbie Lucas, Heather Nolan and Christine Whitley for their advice and encouragement, and, most especially, my wife and daughter, Jenny and Josie, for their help and support in the writing of this book.

Some notes on sources

The poem on p 249 is 'The Price of Experience' by William Blake. Although it was first published in *The Writings of William Blake* (eds Edwin J. Ellis and William Butler Yeats, 1893) it was written in 1797, so it's not impossible to imagine that someone who knew Blake personally, a character similar to Tom Shepherd, in fact, would have seen it.

Parts of the conversations on pp 136–7 and 181–2 were inspired by passages in *The British Tar in Fact and Fiction* by Commander Charles N. Robertson (Harper and Brothers, London, 1911). These capture the language of the era so wonderfully I did not want to change them beyond recognition.

Although I was determined to base the characters and their circumstances firmly in historic reality, *Powder Monkey* is first and foremost a novel rather than a history book. For any reader wanting to find out more about the real history here, I can recommend any of the following:

Jack Aubrey Commands: An Historical Companion to the Naval World of Patrick O'Brian by Brian Lavery (Conway Maritime Press, London, 2003)

The Seafarers: Fighting Sail by A.B.C. Whipple and the editors of Time-Life Books (Caxton Publishing Group, London, 2004)

Hornblower's Navy: Life at Sea in the Age of Nelson by Steve Pope (Orion Books, London, 1998)

Life in Nelson's Navy by Dudley Pope (Chatham Publishing, London,1981)

These are all accessible, highly readable books, which should be available in most public libraries. The first three are also full of fascinating and colourful illustrations – some from the era, others artwork recreations.

If you want to dig a little deeper you could try:

Nelson's Navy: The Ships, Men and Organisation 1793–1815 by Brian Lavery (Conway Maritime Press, London, 1989)

The Wooden World: An Anatomy of the Georgian Navy by N.A.M. Rodger (Collins, London, 1986)

Sea Life in Nelson's Time by John Masefield (Leo Cooper, 2002 – first published 1905)

The Star Captains: Frigate Command in the Napoleonic Wars by Tom Wareham (Chatham Publishing, London, 2001)

The Sea Warriors by Richard Woodman (Constable Publishers, London, 2001)

The Merchant Navy by Captain A.G. Course (Frederick Muller, London, 1963)

Real enthusiasts could trawl the second-hand book shops for:

The British Tar in Fact and Fiction by Commander Charles N. Robertson (Harper and Brothers, London, 1911)

Memoirs of a Seafaring Life by William Spavens (facsimile edition published by the Folio Society, London, 2004 – originally published in 1796)

Books aside, there's nothing like a trip to a real fighting ship from the era to get a flavour of what life must have been like aboard. British readers can visit the frigate HMS *Trincomalee* in Hartlepool – upon which the *Miranda* is closely based (see www.hms-trincoma lee.co.uk), and Nelson's famous flagship HMS *Victory* in Portsmouth. The *Victory*'s excellent website (www.hms-victory.com) includes a list of all 820 men serving on the ship during the Battle of Trafalgar, together with their age, nationality and position.

North American readers can visit another frigate from the era, USS *Constitution*, berthed in Boston, Massachusetts (see www.ussconstitution.navy.mil).

And finally…

Peter Weir's *Master and Commander* film (2003), starring Russell Crowe as Patrick O'Brian's character Captain Jack Aubrey, painstakingly recreates a frigate similar to HMS *Miranda*. It's a rip-roaring action adventure too!

Read on for a sneak peek at *Prison Ship,* a thrilling new Sam Witchall adventure!

A mere six weeks after Sam Witchall's ship wrecked off the Cornish coast in March 1801, Sam has rejoined the Navy as a powder monkey. But his hopes for a second chance at sea are dashed when he and his friend Richard are framed for cowardice during battle. Will they be able to prove their innocence? Or will Sam and Richard find themselves facing a more terrifying future than the hangman's noose? Find out in this exciting new adventure that details every nail-biting moment of Sam Witchall's life as a young sailor.

CHAPTER 3

The Battle of Copenhagen

That night my sleep was constantly disturbed by the sound of ice bumping against the hull of the *Elephant*. The temperature was so cold that when a man carrying a lantern made his way through the deck you could see his breath curling like smoke from his nose and mouth. Water dripped from the low wooden ceiling and condensation settled like dew, chilling me to the marrow.

Breakfast burgoo and scotch coffee never tasted better. I wondered why the body craved sweet things when it was cold. James had told me about a dried fruit and brown sugar delicacy the Scots called 'black bun', which they fried in batter in a deep pan of oil. It sounded just right for a day like this.

As we ate I asked Tom what he thought our tactics would be. He paused between mouthfuls then said, 'We've all seen that row of Danish ships. I reckon we're gonna squeeze up next to them and slug it out. We'll be so close we won't be able to miss.'

I lost my appetite. But James offered me a crumb of comfort.

'We're used to fighting, whereas the Danes aren't scrappers. Whatever happens I'll bet we'll be firing at least twice as quickly as them. So our 74s 'll be like 148 gun ships to them. And their 74s, if they've got any, will be like our frigates. I think we'll make short work of it.'

John Giddes looked sceptical and put in a rare word. 'Most of those Danish ships 've had their masts taken down. They're probably grounded in the mud, so there's no retreat for them. We might 'ave better ships, better guns and better commanders, but we're still foreigners here. The Danes are fightin' for their lives and for their city so I don't think they're gonna be a walkover.'

Giddes was acting as though the incident last night had never happened, but he refused to meet my eye. I wanted to talk to Tom and Richard about him, and what I had heard, but so far I hadn't had the chance.

* * *

Talk around the table dried up. As I finished my burgoo knocked back the dregs of my coffee I wondered if this was the last meal I would ever eat? After breakfast we were called out on deck so the Reverend Eaves could hold a brief service. I peered through the cold morning light at this short, thickset man in his clerical robes, and strained to hear him speak.

Almighty and everlasting God, mercifully look upon
  our infirmities,
And in all our dangers and necessities,
Stretch forth thy right hand to help and defend us;
Through Jesus Christ our Lord, Amen.

The words consoled me, although I couldn't help but wonder whether the Danes were reciting exactly the same prayers too, and whether their infirmities, dangers and necessities would be looked upon any less mercifully by the Almighty.

The ship was called to quarters and we scattered sand on the decks to soak up the blood that was sure to be spilt. Richard pointed out that much of our fleet were still at their anchor to the North, and wondered why they were not closer. 'Too many ships, too little space,' I said. I was glad Richard would be close to me in the battle. I liked to think we would be able to look out for each other. I hoped I would not be called upon to throw him over the side if he were terribly injured.

We waited in silence by our gun, growing tense and numb. Being out in the open the quarterdeck was much colder than the gun decks, and I longed to be down there under cover. The wind rattled the netting that had been placed above our heads to protect us from any yardarms that might fall when fighting started. It was an uncomfortable reminder of how dangerous it was out here. My experience of battle had taught me first hand that enemy ships always aimed at our masts and rigging to try to cripple us. And here on the quarterdeck we were also easy targets for snipers up in the enemy's fighting tops – something we had never had to worry about on the gun deck. Worst of all, with all those disadvantages, we were close to the middle of the ship – the spot where the enemy always concentrated his fire. During any battle, I'd heard it said, most of those killed were from the middle of the ship. My eyes began to water in the face of that wind. I hoped no one would think I was crying in fear.

Just after ten o' clock the rumble of cannon fire rolled across the water. The battle was finally beginning and I would soon be able to forget about the wind and the cold. At once we were called over to the larboard guns and waited for our ship to move into action. The harbour guns were flashing in the middle distance, although their shot was falling short. Gun smoke began to drift across the water towards us and catch in our throats.

For the first time, I could see what a battle looked like rather than just hear and feel it. On the gun deck of my old ship, the *Miranda*, we could only tell what was happening by listening to the commands of our officers. Once the firing started, with the roar of the cannons and the ringing in our ears, even that became impossible.

For now, seeing events unfolding from the quarterdeck was thrilling – like watching a forbidden play or hearing a fascinating conversation not meant for our ears. But I also felt terribly exposed. It was like a dream I sometimes had where I stood naked in the congregation at a christening or wedding.

We watched our ships slowly move towards the Danish line. HMS *Edgar* was first to edge forward along a narrow stretch of water in front of the enemy. I did not envy them their task. As soon as she reached the Danes their muzzles flashed in the grey morning light. There was something random and ill-judged about the Danish barrage. Their gunners were obviously not men who had trained every day, as we had.

In reply the *Edgar* unleashed a thunderous, ordered broadside. Splinters flew into the air and peppered the sea, as the first ship in the Danish line was ravaged by her cannon fire. But as the *Edgar* sailed down the enemy line she began to take fire too. Before she dropped anchor in front of the fifth ship in the line, several of the Danish guns had found their target. I could barely bring myself to look as splinters burst from the *Edgar*'s wooden walls. It was easy to imagine the carnage left in the wake of the shot as it tore through her decks. Two more of our ships followed behind the the *Edgar* to take up their positions opposite Danish vessels.

As two further 74s followed, disaster struck. On their approach to the narrow channel, they grounded in the shallows. But they carried on firing from where they had halted and their shot was hitting home. Then another of our ships moved forward but she too was caught on the Middle Ground before she could even reach the channel. I wondered if Spavens had taken the wrong soundings on our trip the night before. Now, all of a sudden, the battle was turning against us.

'Let fall' came the order. Our sails filled and the

Elephant edged forward. It was our turn to brave the fire of the Danish line and I struggled to keep my fear at bay. It was time to stop watching and start taking part. We sailed before the wind and I wondered if we too would be grounded. But the *Elephant* carried on moving forward and we were soon within range of our enemies. Shots from the shore batteries began to scream down around us. They landed fore and aft, throwing up plumes of water or whistling close by the sails and rigging. The fire was fierce but none hit home and we sailed on without damage.

As we approached the Danish ships I began to feel something close to terror. Standing there in the open, clutching my cartridge box, I expected at any moment to be hit and vanish in a fiery, bloody flash. James could see the fear in my eyes and placed a hand on my shoulder. 'Hold fast Sam, hold fast.'

We reached the first enemy ship and the gunnery officer shouted, 'Fire at will'. Our carronade exploded into life, lurching back on its wooden runner. The 32lb shot made a terrible mess of the quarterdeck of the ship opposite.

'That's why they call it the smasher,' yelled James. No sooner had we fired than Tom, James, Vincent and Richard began swabbing out and reloading. I handed over my cartridge, relieved not to be holding something that could blow me into tiny pieces, and then ran for all my worth down the four staircases that led to the after powder room in the hold. Grabbing another cartridge I stuffed it in my box, screwed the lid down tight and was back before Tom and his crew could fire again.

'Well done Sam,' said Tom. 'Hold fast now, we'll be firing any second.' I could barely hear him over the noise of the guns.

Each Danish ship passed before us, close enough for me to see their crew. Muskets cracked from their masts, and shots thudded down on to our deck. Close by, one of the marines clutched his shoulder and fell backwards, his musket clattering to the deck and discharging its ball. It buried itself in the wooden rail close by our carronade. I said a silent prayer of thanks. To be shot by one of our own men would have been inglorious.

I thanked God too that we were wearing our dull sailor's slops and not the bright red jackets of the marines. Even through the smoke of battle they made an easy target here on our deck, as did the officers in their blue jackets and gold braid.

Each Danish ship fired its long guns at us as we passed, but the fire was slapdash. Tom was right. The Danes were unskilled in handling their guns. Again our carronade exploded into life. The shot hit home, crashing into the foremast of a Danish 74, causing several men in the fighting top to fall to the deck. Now I could see the work of our gun as it mauled ships and claimed lives with every discharge, I wished again that I was down in the gun deck as I had been on the *Miranda*. But then a sliver of shot landed right at my foot, missing my cartridge box and my toes by a fraction of an inch. That fired me up. 'Give the bastards one from me, Tom,' I said before I ran off to collect more powder.

We passed a dozen or so of their ships, all firing as the *Elephant* moved forward. Then came the order to stop. Across the sea from us was the *Dannebrog*, so close we could see the men on her deck, even through the gun smoke.

'She's a 60 by the look of her,' said Tom, 'and she's flyin' the Danish admiral's flag.'

Over the top of the gun port I could see she was a handsome man-o'-war, tall in the water and bristling with cannon along her two gun decks and quarterdeck. She was also badly damaged, having suffered the attentions of the British ships who had passed down their line before us.

My ears began to ring from the sound of cannon fire. I was glad of it as I could no longer hear the screams of injured men. Immediately to our stern was HMS *Glatton*, which I had learned was commanded by the notorious Captain Bligh, but I could barely see her through the gun smoke, nor any of the other ships who fought alongside us.

Our carronade fired constantly and I began to tire of my incessant trips to the powder room. The Danish forces, though formidable, seemed to be doing little damage to the *Elephant*. Perhaps we'd been lucky for now.

The battle continued; more of our ships took up position in front of the Danish fleet. Through the smoke I saw a squadron of frigates pass down the line behind us. Although we pounded her steadily, the *Dannebrog* continued to fire back.

As we fought, Lord Nelson walked up and down the quarterdeck behind us – excitedly urging us on. He seemed unconcerned for his safety, and his courage gave me heart. When a shot hit the mainmasts and showered us with splinters I heard him say to an officer, 'It is warm work, and this day may be the last for any of us at a moment.' Then he laughed and said, 'Mark you, I would not be elsewhere for thousands!' I could not agree. I would have *given* thousands to be elsewhere.

As a musket shot whistled over my head I heard a midshipman rush up to inform Lord Nelson that Hyde Parker had hoisted a signal ordering him to break off the action. I wondered at first how such a signal could be seen, but perhaps the view was clearer atop our masts? 'Thank the Lord,' I thought. 'Let's get away from here before we're all killed.'

I ran to the magazine hoping fervently this would be the last cartridge I would have to fetch for this battle, and by the time I returned we would be calling off the action. But when I got back, Nelson and Captain Foley had come close to the rail by our cannon and I heard almost all of what they said.

'You know Foley,' said Lord Nelson, 'I have only one eye – I have a right to be blind sometimes.' Then he put his telescope to his blind eye, turned it towards Hyde Parker's ship and said, 'I really do not see the signal.'

I had to bite my tongue. I wanted to scream 'Don't be stupid. Do what you have been ordered you to do!

What if the Swedish and Russian fleets are coming?' But I knew such insolence could get me flogged to death or hanged. What had made Hyde Parker make such a signal, though? Whenever I could, I squinted through the smoke to see if there were any more masts on the horizon.

As midday turned to early afternoon the *Dannebrog* began to burn steadily and acrid smoke drifted towards. I could also see that several of the Danish ships had surrendered. Some burned fiercely. I wondered if their magazines would explode and cause carnage on the neighbouring ship in the Danish line. Aboard the blazing ships the sailors who had survived our merciless barrage were trying to escape by throwing themselves from the gun ports or over the side of the upper deck. Some of our ships had launched their boats to try to rescue these poor wretches. Many of them were badly injured and struggled pitifully in the freezing water. But even as we tried to rescue their seamen the Danes still fired upon us from their shore batteries.

Then the *Dannebrog* struck her colours to surrender. All at once I began to breath a little easier and allowed myself to hope I would come out of this battle alive. We were ordered to stop firing, and I sat down on the carriage of the carronade to drink some water. I realised with a twinge of guilt that Lord Nelson had been right not to withdraw. He had sensed, far earlier than me, that we were winning.

Bosun's whistles peeped as some of the *Elephant's* boats were lowered to cross over the narrow stretch of water between us and the *Dannebrog* to help the men who were trying to escape a fiery death. But as they approached they were fired upon with muskets. Lord Nelson, clearly angered, ordered us to start firing again as soon as our boats were out of danger. Vincent Thomas loaded grapeshot into the maw of our carronade and we peppered their deck.

Just after the carronade discharged, while my ears were still ringing, I was thrown to my feet by a violent explosion. When I got up I could see enemy shot had hit the quarterdeck between two guns just down from us and men from the crews were lying dead or dying. They were swiftly picked up by their comrades and thrown over the side. Most of those were beyond caring, but one of them, almost sliced in two by grapeshot, was a young boy who had been powder monkey to the gun next to us. He was clutching at a gaping hole in his belly, trying to stop his insides pouring out, and livid fear danced in his eyes. When they picked him up he started yelling, 'Mother, help me! God help me! Mother, don't let them do this to me ...' The marines hesitated, then their sergeant came over and shouted at them: 'He's a goner. Let him go over and finish him.' They swung the boy as they threw him, which must have hurt him terribly and he screamed all the way down to the water.

I had seen many men die horribly in battle, but this was the worst. That could have been me, howling in agony for my mother. A lieutenant on the quarterdeck swiftly reordered the gun crews from whoever was left alive. Richard was told to act as powder monkey for the carronade next to ours. He was handed the leather cartridge box that the dead boy had been using, and flinched when he saw there was blood all over one side of it.

'I'll show you the drill,' I shouted. 'Whatever happens, keep the lid firmly down. Now follow me.'

We sprinted down the stairwell and ran through the middle of the upper gun deck to the stern. The noise was deafening, the heat unbearable. Then another ladder took us to the lower deck and immediately down to the orlop deck beneath the waterline. From there it was just a few steps to the after powder room. No one else was outside, not even the marine who usually stood guard there. 'Sometimes you have to wait with several powder boys,' I said, 'sometimes not. We're lucky this time.' Then I called for a cartridge and a hand appeared through the wet curtains that shielded the men inside from flying sparks. Richard did the same. As I made sure his lid was screwed tight, Oliver Pritchard came running up to us.

'You two, drop your boxes and follow me now,' he said. We looked at each other in puzzlement, but an order was an order. He said, 'Quickly, down the ladder to the hold.' We did as we were asked. He did not follow. Instead he stood at the top of the ladder and shouted, 'Macintosh, come here at once.' Then he turned to us and drew his pistol. A marine, bayonet on the end of his musket, arrived at his shoulder.

'Caught these two trying to hide in the hold,' he said to the soldier. 'Lock them in the bread room and make sure they stay there.' He tossed the soldier a key and marched off.

'But we were ordered down here,' said Richard.

'And we need to get back to the quarterdeck with our powder,' I shouted.

The marine waved his bayonet at us. 'Shut up or I'll run this through the pair of you.'

We were bundled into the store room and left there in the dark. 'What will our crews do without us?' said Richard. He sounded scared. I felt utterly bewildered.

It was bizarre being in the heat of battle one moment, then the next being locked away from it all at the bottom of the ship. My heart was beating fast and I was bursting with energy. I just had to sit there in the dark with the stifling smell of mouldy bread in my nostrils.

There beneath the waterline we could still hear the muffled discharges of the guns, and more clearly, from the orlop deck above us, the screams of men brought down to the ship's surgeon.

'What the hell is this all about?' Richard said angrily. It was too dark to actually see him.

I began to think more clearly and grew suddenly afraid. Of what I was not quite sure, but I knew we were in terrible trouble.

'I didn't tell you about last night. We've not had time to talk,' I said. 'You know I was gone a while fetching that tobacco. I overheard Nathaniel Pritchard and John Giddes arguing. They were both drunk, and were talking about charges for clothes and tobacco they would take from dead men's wages.

'And then, when they were quarrelling, Pritchard said something to Giddes about him not being who he says he is.'

'Well, we all thought that,' said Richard. 'So who the hell is he?'

'I didn't hear that much –' Then I understood in an instant what was happening to us.

'Oh Jesus Christ help us,' I wailed, crushed by a terrible certainty.

Richard was alarmed. 'What? What is it?'

'Last night – Giddes came to the door. Caught me standing there. I said I'd just arrived and didn't hear a thing. That must have given me away. Now Pritchard has got his son involved, and they're trying to set us up.'

'Why me?' said Richard. His voice seemed angry, even accusatory, as if it was my fault.

Now I felt angry with him. 'Oh, I don't know. Maybe it was because you were here with me just now, maybe they thought I'd tell you anyway. They'd know we were friends.'

Silence fell between us. The battle above our heads was winding down. Only occasional cannon fire could be heard and no one was screaming on the surgeon's table. It was so dark in there neither of us could see our hands in front of our faces.

Richard spoke again. 'So what happens next? We get court-martialled. If we're lucky, we'll be flogged, probably severely. If were unlucky, we get hanged from the yardarm.'

Paul Dowswell

is a former editor as well as the author or co-author of more than fifty acclaimed nonfiction books for children on historical and scientific topics. He lives in Wolverhampton, England, with his wife and daughter. *Powder Monkey* is his first work of fiction.